WAITING FOR THE AARDVARK

Jo Thomson

First Published in Great Britain in 2015
by Jo Thomson

ISBN-13: 978-1514239513

ISBN-10: 1514239515

My sincere thanks to Maz Moldon and Phill Turner, without whom this would not have been possible.

And thank you to those who believed in me, you know who you are.

You never gave me chance to say goodbye.

You never let me wave that final time.

You never held me close before we parted

Or warned that we might break before my heart did.

I re-live that final day

How we talked short hours away

But you never gave me a chance to say...

Goodbye.

J.T.

Chapter 1

I stared at my best friend, in anticipation of her response, and for a few moments she stared back at me. Finally, she broke the silence.

'Alison, you are *such* a stupid cow!'

With those profound words, we both gave in to helpless laughter and Hilary reached for the wine.

'I know I am, but I got backed into a corner. What else could I say, but yes?'

'Well, "no" might have been a better option!' She giggled into her wine and started spluttering.

'It's not funny,' I said, trying, not altogether successfully, to keep a straight face. 'What the hell am I going to do about it?'

At last she pulled herself together, while I waited, hopefully, for the person who had shared every dream and nightmare I'd ever had to come up with some miraculous solution to the crazy situation I had managed to create for myself.

'He's going to stay with you for the whole of the summer holidays?'

'Yes. All eight weeks.'

'Derek *and* both his children?'

'Yes.' I attempted to maintain a sulky expression.

Finally, still chewing her lip to fight off further giggles, she shrugged and said, 'I guess you must really like him, then.'

'Well, obviously I like him!' I looked away, thinking for a moment. 'I do. I may be a stupid cow, but if I didn't really like him, I'd have said no straight away and found a suitable excuse later.'

She smiled at me, the laughter gone. She smiled with the compassion that I had come to rely upon so much over the years. The expression that said, I know what you're going through and I'll do anything I can to help.

'But he's not Rob, is he?' she said, at last.

I shook my head, feeling the tell-tale prickle in my eyes.

'Have you heard from him?'

I shook my head again and gulped a large quantity of wine. 'No, and I won't ever hear from him again. The letter said it all and said goodbye.' I took a deep breath and attempted a convincing, strong-willed glare. 'Rob is history. And anyway, that letter was nearly two years ago.'

'But it's not as if Derek's suddenly going to be the first man who's stayed over since then, is it?'

'No one has actually *stayed*, as such. And no one's brought their kids with them either!' I added, somewhat sourly. 'Anyway, that's not the point. It isn't some sort of hang-up about having a relationship 'post-Rob' - I do need a life - but this is different.'

Hilary gave me a whimsical smile and got up to fetch another bottle of wine so we could keep the alcohol therapy flowing.

'I know this is different. It could be getting serious, couldn't it?'

'I don't know.'

'It sounds as if Derek might be trying to make it serious.'

'That's what worries me.'

'It sounds as if you do know, then.'

I shook my head and held out my glass.

She overfilled both glasses and the grin started to spread across her face again.

'You know, if I *had* to, I could list all the men you've slept with since Rob, and I could probably also give them your comparative marks out of ten – not, I hasten to add, that you talk about it much...'

'And you don't?' I retorted.

'We're not talking about me.'

'Oh? Is there someone you're not telling me about?'

'*No*, there isn't and don't even think about trying to change the subject!'

I grinned at her look of determination. 'Anyway, what do you mean, *all* the men since Rob – there's only been two.'

Hilary cocked her head questioningly.

I thought for a moment. 'Oh. Okay, three. I forgot Derek.'

With that, she burst out laughing. It took me a second to realize what I'd said, and then I became as helpless as she was.

'*Oops*,' I said, after we'd both returned to something like normality. 'Actually, Derek is the only one that really counts as *after* Rob.'

Hilary looked at me quite seriously. 'Once Rob appeared there never really was a *before* that meant anything, was

3

there? And you never believed there'd be an *after* either, did you?'

I shook my head, unable to say anything, but all too aware of the tears in my eyes again.

After what seemed like a long time, both of us sipping our wine in silence, I glanced up at her.

'Since we seem to be intent on discussing my sex life,' I began, with an attempt at flippancy, 'I guess the other two – the only other two ever – don't really count.'

Hilary tried to match my mood. 'This is where I say, What about Mark? And you reply, Mark is just Mark!'
'Well, he is.'

'Ally,' she said, with a look of frustration, 'you and Mark were made for each other.'

'Mark and I are just great friends—'

'Friends that sleep together?' she interrupted.

'Oh, Hilary, you know the score. We work together virtually every day – we have done for six years. Sometimes we go out for a drink, or a meal, to celebrate or commiserate over a job. We can talk about everything – the good stuff and the bad. It's just that on a few occasions the bad things have needed…I don't know…comforting.'

She smiled. 'You may be only workmates, but he probably knows as much about you and your life as I do.'

I nodded.

'And he knew all about Rob.'

'Yes. I probably used him to fill the gaps where Rob wasn't.'

'I'm sure he knew that and he still worships the ground you walk on.'

'Now you have lost it! He's totally besotted with some actress, at the moment. In fact I'm beginning to be fed up with the sound of her name.'

I sensed my friend watching me, but I refused to look at her.

'Did Rob know about Mark?'

'Good God, no!' Momentarily, unwillingly, I let myself go back. 'Rob had horrendous double standards. He believed in fidelity.'

Hilary snorted.

'Yes, I know.' I shrugged. 'At first I totally agreed, because, in a way, we were faithful to each other. He had a wife who wouldn't sleep with him, but he still believed in his children and the whole family unit thing. I suppose I was just the part of his life that was missing. To him that was acceptable. And it was to me, then. I've never felt like that about anyone. I doubt I ever will again.' I stared into my glass. 'I suppose, eventually, I realized it wasn't enough for me and Mark filled a gap occasionally, but I could never have told Rob.'

'He never would have left her, would he?'

'At the beginning I was so sure he would, but no, probably not.'

Finally I looked up at Hilary. She didn't have to remind me how hard it still was to admit to that.

We drained that bottle and Hilary opened a third, but she wasn't quite finished with the interrogation.

'Does Derek know about Mark?'

'Only that we work together and that we're friends.'

'So what happens if Mark's actress dumps him in the next couple of weeks and Mark needs…er…comforting?'

'That would be sod's law, wouldn't it!'

I grabbed a huge handful of peanuts to soak up some of the alcohol. We should have been reeling from two bottles of wine, but even with the laughter returning, there was a sober atmosphere in the room. Not, however, totally sober.

Suddenly Hilary said, 'And what about Kris?'

Before I had a chance to reply, she went on, 'God, with a name like that, he *had* to become a country music singer!'

'I know. His dad wanted to call him Waylon.'

'You're joking?'

'No, seriously. I think he only plays in our band to fulfil his father's childhood ambition.'

'Well, he's pretty good at it.'

'He's *brilliant*.'

'Are we still talking about music?'

Sobriety vanished and laughter took hold again.

I poured myself a ridiculously large glass of wine and turned to face Hilary, stating, with as much melodrama as I could manage, 'You know, he was my first love.'

'I do,' Hilary responded. 'If your dads had had the remotest idea what their teenage kids were getting up to, I don't know who would have been strangled first.'

'My dad would have died of shock!'

'So, what about Kris? He's stayed since Rob, hasn't he?'

'Oh, come on, you know as well as I do that it's probably only a throwback from our teenage years. If it hadn't happened then, it would never have happened again. Anyway, it's only been a couple of times, when we were still on a high after a gig.'

She looked at me, with a feigned look of innocence. 'And haven't you got a gig in a couple of weeks?'

When the laughter finally subsided, we sat without speaking for a few minutes, both still with silly smiles on our faces.

After a while, Hilary asked, 'Has Derek got the whole school holidays off work?'

'No, otherwise they'd all be at his place. He's got some consultancy thing to do, only about five miles from me. That's how this stupid idea came up in the first place. He reckons he can get odd days off most weeks, and then, at some point, time to have a proper holiday.'

'So what usually happens in the summer, when he goes to work?'

'Often they have camps and things to go to, or he manages to fob them off with friends' parents for a few days. If that doesn't work, I suppose he must take them with him. I'm not sure really. I didn't know him that well last summer.'

'No grandparents?'

'Only on their mother's side and they don't want to know. I get the impression they've never been very interested, even when she was alive.'

'Maybe he thinks you can look after them.'

'He can bloody well think again! Mind you, I did say I'd take them to work a couple of times, pay them some pittance, if they want to do some painting or stuff.'

'You did dig a hole for yourself, didn't you?'

'Didn't I just!'

I reached for my glass, but it was beginning to get to me now and I felt an increasingly urgent need for coffee.

'Hopefully, he'll take them away on holiday somewhere, after the first couple of weeks.' I grimaced at a sudden recollection. 'Although he did mutter something about *us* going away!'

'How many does *us* amount to?'

'Four,' I replied, with a pained expression.

Hilary's grin returned. 'When do they start calling you Mum?'

'Bloody never!'

'And what are you going to do about your social life?'

'What do you mean?'

'Well, band practice, the gym, our nights out.'

'I'm not going to stop doing all that,' I answered, feeling quite annoyed at the suggestion that I might.

'Does Derek know that?'

'He'll find out, won't he?'

'Are you sure this idea of them staying is just because Derek's going to be working nearby?'

I waited.

'I mean, could this be a trial period?' she said, quite seriously.

I felt my eyes widen, involuntarily.

'The kids are, what, eleven and fifteen? Difficult ages without a mother, especially for a teenage daughter.'

The effect of the wine seemed to drain away in an instant. I stared out of the window, into the night. 'I have never wanted to be a mother,' I said soberly, 'and I'm *not* about to start now.'

Chapter 2

I arrived at work with more than just the trace of a headache. It wasn't the first time, after staying at Hilary's and putting the world to rights. I had the distinct feeling that it wouldn't be the last either, before I made it through the next eight weeks.

I let myself in to the house where we were currently working and went straight to the kitchen to put on the kettle. There was a note on the table from the home owners. I was reading it as the doorbell rang.

'How's the head?' Mark inquired, as I let him in. The effects of three bottles of wine were evidently obvious.

'Not as bad as Hilary's, I hope.'

He took over putting tea bags in cups, while I finished reading the note. 'Do you want the good news or the bad news?'

'There's no milk?' he suggested.

'That wouldn't be bad news, that'd be disastrous.'

'Not for you, it wouldn't, you'd make me go and get some.'

'True!'

'Here you are.' He handed me a mug of tea. 'Got your own Paracetamol?'

'Already taken. Well, they think everything is looking brilliant. So brilliant, in fact, and we're obviously such good workers, that could we please go ahead and put in the outside tap that they decided could wait last week, *and* box in all the pipes in the study as well.'

'And then just decorate the study, by any chance?'

'That's probably tomorrow's note.'

'We're not here tomorrow.'

'We are now!'

I stood finishing my tea, inwardly dreading the phone call to the client who thought we would be arriving at her house in the morning. She had already put up with a delayed start, as this job had grown since we arrived. I made a mental note to build in time gaps between jobs, wondering exactly how many times I had promised myself to do that.

Mark plonked his empty cup down. 'Okay, what's the first job?'

'You put the locks in the lounge doors and I'll finish plastering the fireplace. Then, in theory, we put up those last three wall units in the kitchen, clear up and go home.'

'The theory sounds good,' he muttered.

I smiled. 'That bit usually is. And I'd lay money that they don't decorate any of it themselves. I bet we're back here in a couple of months.'

'Oh well, keeps us off the streets.'

'Speak for yourself,' I said with a grin, 'I might like a change of profession!'

*

By mid-afternoon the house was clean, tidy and empty of all our tools, which had been residing in their cupboard under the stairs for the past three weeks.

'Can we nip out now, get the gear and finish the other bits tonight?' Mark asked.

I looked at my watch and ran through the time we'd need to get it all done.

'No,' I answered, after a moment. 'If we had the stuff here, we could probably just about do it, but we'd lose too much time going to and from suppliers, and besides, I've got band practice tonight.'

'Okay, it was only a thought.'

'Why are you so keen to work late anyway? I'll have to pay you for another day here if we come back tomorrow.'

'It was just an idea. Melanie's got some audition for a play this evening.'

'Ah, poor, lonely Mark. Try finding yourself a life for when she's not around!'

'You don't understand,' he retorted. 'You don't care about Derek in the same way.'

I shook my head. 'No, you're right, I kind of wish I did.'

He gave me a sympathetic smile. 'Shall we have another cup of tea?'

'Good idea.'

*

I found time, on my way home, to buy the materials necessary for the morning and swung into my driveway with long lengths of MDF board propped up against the back of the passenger seat, threatening to slide across into my left ear. At least, this evening, I could leave everything in there. I didn't have to create a space to add a guitar to the chaos. Band practice was at my house.

The house was empty of brothers. Phil, the eldest, usually had an after-school club for his 1st rugby fifteen on a Wednesday, and Andy…well, Andy could be anywhere. Feeling, as usual, as if I had left one building site to return to another, I jumped over a couple of bags of plaster that might, or might not, be used in one of the many half-finished rooms at the weekend, cleared a pile of papers off my office chair and picked up the phone.

Having grovelled an apology to a long-suffering pensioner, whose bedroom was not about to be redecorated the next morning, I gave myself a pat on the back for managing to talk my way out of working Friday. It would seem a bit disruptive to start for one day and then leave for the weekend – sorry again! At least now I had a bit more time to prepare for Derek and the kids arriving on Saturday. That thought sent me straight into the lounge to pour a large drink.

I caught sight of myself in the mirror: short, blonde hair, now tinged slightly pink with plaster dust. I stopped to consider that perhaps my size 12 T-shirt was a bit too tight, but I'd got served very quickly in the timber yard, and the guy had been eager to help me out to the car with the stuff, so maybe it wasn't such a bad thing. Suddenly I remembered Hilary's reaction to my news and chuckled at my reflection. 'Alison, she's right. You *are* a stupid cow!'

I took the drink to the bath, hoping both lots of liquid would clear away the strains of the day.

The front door slammed and Andy called out, 'Hi! Only me!' as his footsteps pounded up the stairs.

I leaned over and pushed my bathroom door to. 'I've got band practice here tonight,' I shouted.

'I know. Anyway, I'm out.'

'Glad you're finding a social life, at last!'

'Put your head under the water and count to five hundred,' he instructed, as he walked past towards his own bathroom.

Before I'd managed to drag myself out of the bath, I heard footsteps going past again, in the opposite direction this time. 'Bye,' he shouted, 'see you tomorrow.'

*

I'd barely finished eating when the doorbell rang. It would be the two men. Kris and Craig always arrived together, always early. Jane was always late.

'Hi,' they greeted me, shuffling in with various instruments and cans of beer. They made their way into the lounge, leaving me to make a pretence of clearing away my dinner – the dishwasher *might* get loaded later – and then run upstairs to grab my guitar. When I came down, both were sitting with cowboy hats on their heads. I burst out laughing.

'Well, we are playing the interval for a barn dance,' Craig said.

'Are you serious?'

'Yes. Why not?'

I looked at the pair of them for a moment. 'Actually, I think I like it.'

'Thank God for that,' Kris replied, 'or I've just wasted thirty quid.' He reached down and produced two more hats, jumped to his feet and pushed one on my head. 'Hey, it looks good,' he said. 'I don't know why we haven't done this before.'

The bell rang again and Craig got up to answer, grabbing the spare hat from Kris. When he returned both he and Jane were wearing them at a rakish angle.

'Sorry guys,' she announced, 'I forgot the jeans and checked shirt.'

We all exchanged glances, with a grin.

'Solves this gig's clothes problem,' Kris said.

We tuned up, played, sang and drank large quantities of beer – all except Craig, that is, who was driver for the night. We rotated the venue for practices, and had worked out a system of giving lifts and staying that meant one person had to remain completely sober only once every four weeks. That short straw carried with it the responsibility of directing the evening's rehearsal and taking notes about changes to various parts and harmonies. We all considered we were frightfully democratic.

Craig looked down his list. 'Ally, it's up to you – are we going to include this next song in the set? Only you weren't happy with the guitar part last week and we haven't got long to make a final decision.'

I took a deep breath. 'Yes, *definitely*,' the confidence of the beer announced. 'Use this as a final dress rehearsal. If it doesn't work we'll drop it, but it will be brilliant. After all, I put in a massive ten minutes' practice on Sunday!'

'Oh, a whole five minutes more than me,' Jane muttered.

'Don't mock, you've got a fiddle part to try out afterwards!' Craig informed her haughtily.

Jane and I exchanged amused glances. 'God, he's a pain in the arse when he's in charge.'

I took another gulp of beer, another deep breath, made a momentary plea to my guitar to work well with me and glanced at Kris, who was singing the melody, for reassurance. Some four minutes later we ended in perfect harmony, and I played my last half dozen notes to complete the song. No one said a word. Finally I had to grin like the proverbial Cheshire cat. 'Yes!' I said quietly, with a tiny punch at the air.

At that moment the door opened and my brother, Phil, poked his head into the room. 'Marty Robbins would be proud of you,' he said, and retreated again.

Kris was smiling broadly. It was just a song, only one song, but it was a guitar part I had been promising myself I would learn for years. I doubted that half the barn dance participants would even have heard of 'El Paso', but it was special for me, and it mattered to me that Kris knew that.

'That's a definite, then,' Craig said, writing on his notepad. 'Okay, Jane, so how is that fiddle part going?'

The session broke up at about ten thirty. The men packed up their gear and finally left after a cursory clearance of all the beer cans and general agreement on the next practice night. I made coffee for myself and Jane, who was staying the night, and Phil joined us for a brandy nightcap.

16

'It's all sounding pretty good,' he said. 'Well, through closed doors and not having to look at you, anyway!'

Chapter 3

My head had told me that today would only be half a day's work, at most, but my instinct was just beginning to question that. I was squashed in a ridiculous position under the sink, with my bum sticking up in the air. My hair was wet from the residue of water in a pipe, and now covered in dust from trying to drill a hole in a very hard wall with a very blunt drill bit. Suddenly it broke through, and a waft of foul-smelling air greeted me from the outside gully. I clambered backwards out of the sink unit, and used the worktop to haul myself, and an aching back, upright. It was definitely time for a break.

Mark was upstairs, creating some artistic cover for some ugly heating pipes in the client's study. As a trained bricklayer, he made quite a good carpenter. My father had taken him on shortly before he and my mother had died. I guess he had seen his potential.

I worked for my dad then, as well, but I was the boss's daughter, which was probably why Mark never had a problem accepting me as boss when I took over the business. My dad had always hoped one of his kids would be his successor, but I doubt he envisaged it would be his daughter! Phil had shown no interest at all. He had wanted to teach sports since he was first picked for his school rugby team at thirteen. Andy and I had always been more practical-minded, having had hammers, saws, chisels and other such lethal weapons in our hands since we were kids.

I had completed my A levels at school and then been sent to college to study surveying, building administration, building law and other incredibly boring things. By the time Andy had reached eighteen, I was already begging my father to let me join him and get my hands dirty, learning on the job. Andy had heard all my pleading and flatly refused to even start down the full-time college route, so we both began together as my dad's apprentices, and suffered the boring stuff at day release and evening classes.

Very quickly, Andy decided he would make an excellent plasterer, which he did. I always reckoned it was because he never had his fill of making mud-pies as a kid. He certainly loved any opportunity to make as much mess as possible – even now... I had decided I simply wanted to experience every trade, and I wanted to do what my dad did – be a supervisor. Andy reckoned that was because I was naturally bossy. He walked away from the business at twenty-two and my dad was faced with his one and only heir.

What had made it easy for Mark and me to get along was that we had met as a couple of twenty-something's, both learning the trade. We both took orders, we both grumbled about them, we both got dirty, we both got told off and we could both laugh about it all. That history made him one of the few people in my life who I could accept seeing me in the state I was in right now.

I tipped some water I'd saved in a saucepan into the kettle and shouted up the stairs. 'Mark! Tea!'

He appeared quite quickly, took one look at me and snorted.

'What?'

'You must have had your goggles on.'

'Yes, so?'

'You look like a panda. Everything's grey, except for two circles round your eyes.'

I grinned up at him. He towered above me. He towered above most people. He was big without being at all fat, with curly dark hair and deep dark eyes that had captured mine the first time we had met over a length of drainpipe. I had slipped over in the mud in a trench we had dug out. Mark had reached out to help me up and lost his footing. To this day I swear he did it deliberately. When my dad had appeared to check on his workforce, he found the two of us totally mud-encrusted and giggling like a pair of school kids.

A few months after the mud wrestling incident, that particular house had been completed, ahead of time, with not one single penalty clause incurred. We'd all gone out for a drink. One drink led to another and Mark and I had slipped away. We spent hours talking over a cheap, eat-all-you-can pasta buffet. Eventually the waiter got fed up with delivering more coffee and delivered the bill. It seemed so natural to talk about our lives, our loves, our dreams. It seemed just as natural to get into a taxi and go back to Mark's place. My father never made any comment on the fact that I arrived to work the following day without having been home.

Mark and I just grinned at each other that morning. There were no apologies, no recriminations, no deep conversations about how things could have been if our lives were different right now. I just knew that it wouldn't be the last such evening. There were other houses that would come out of the mud and be completed.

I no longer did the kind of major works that my father had once done, but all the work I now took on included Mark. I simply couldn't imagine not having him there.

The kettle boiled, we drank our tea; he returned to the study, I folded myself back into the sink unit, and soon it was all complete and we were driving our separate routes home.

*

It was a luxury to have a few hours spare. I ate a whole bar of chocolate and sat in the garden, enjoying the solitude and the sunshine. It felt like the height of decadence. Loath to end that mood, I lit a candle in the bathroom and soaked in muscle-relaxing bubbles for over an hour.

My evening meal consisted of something boring but high in carbohydrates, which I dutifully consumed before changing into tracksuit and trainers and heading out to the gym.

I spotted a friend in the car park.

'Hi Ally.'

'Oh, hi, how are you?'

'I'm much better now, thanks.'

'Good to see you back. Are you doing circuit training?'

'Not tonight, but next week, maybe.'

It surprised me. She had had a nasty bout of flu, but she was the keenest keep-fit freak I knew.

I locked the car and headed upstairs, wondering, for the thousandth time, what sadistic mind had decided to open a gym that wasn't on the ground floor, in a building with no lift. The very same sadistic mind met me halfway up the fifteen steps that I'd counted, weekly, for over four years. The reason for my friend's departure then became apparent.

'Oh, Ally, I hoped I'd see you. I've got to go to a meeting, so Jason's taking the class tonight.'

'Ah, Jason!'

'He was the only one available. There are two new youngsters joining tonight, so could you keep an eye on them?'

'What do you mean? Tell them Jason's a prat and it'll be better next week?'

The owner of the gym smiled at me. She and I had become good mates over four years. 'No comment,' she replied.

Jason was twenty-six and a recently qualified PE teacher who knew it all. He had started an athletics club for boys from his school, which was, of course, going to be the best in the area. Rumour had it that he had a couple of international vests for 10,000 metres. He was fitter than most people would ever be, he was also tall and rather gorgeous – which he knew – with perfect muscles in all the right places. The trouble, for me and a few others, was that he arrived to teach with an entourage of his boys – at least half a dozen sixteen-year-old lads, who hung on his every word and turned every exercise into a competition, whether it was supposed to be or not.

I found the two new girls and did my best to make them feel welcome. What I didn't tell them was that I was now going to do my best to screw up Jason's disciples. I think Jason probably enjoyed it, I knew I did. I suspected that he picked the exercises to suit me, but he would never have admitted it.

'Okay,' the keep-fit king announced, after he'd done his best to exhaust everyone with the warm-up, 'this next exercise is just some sprint training. We'll do it teams, so could you divide up into groups of four, please.'

We shuffled around to form our fours. I had done this many times. I knew I was going to go first, and I knew who would be the first in each of the other groups. I wasn't someone with great stamina, but I was devastating over thirty metres; Jason's lads would go on to run marathons, but they couldn't sprint to save their lives. I think Jason was trying to flatten their egos, but it always boosted mine.

'On your marks, get set, go!'

I reached the other end of the gym with a trailing group of annoyed teenagers in my wake. They had just been beaten by someone well over ten years their senior and, worse still, a woman! Jason wasn't my favourite person, but he did wonders for my self-esteem.

As the class ended and I climbed back into my car, I was tired, physically wrung out, but still smiling. If Derek thought I was giving this up for the next eight weeks, he had another think coming!

Chapter 4

I had got on quite well with Derek's children on the few occasions that we had all been together in the past, but the closer the time came to their arrival, the less idea I had of what to do with two kids for a big chunk of the summer. At least on their one previous visit they had loved the house, albeit for very different reasons.

For eleven-year-old Tony, his first impression had been one of utter chaos, which he thought was wonderful. He wasn't being shouted at for making a mess, or told to be strictly on his best behaviour. We did have some respectable rooms, but the majority were – at best – unfinished. An outsider's view would probably have put it as a cross between a run-down farm and a building site. Added to that were the various comings and goings of my two brothers and me, with our own heaps of belongings, hobbies and exceedingly untidy habits. It gave it the feel of an aged students' accommodation block. Tony pronounced it 'really cool'.

Sarah had two reasons to be happy to be here. As quiet and reserved a teenager as she was, her passion for new clothes was just what you would expect from a fifteen-year-old girl and I had – foolishly – told her she might be able to do a few days' work for me, for money. By far her main delight at staying in the house, however, was that she had fallen, instantly, madly in love with my twenty-eight-year-old brother, Andy, at their one and only meeting. I had a feeling she would be severely disillusioned and disappointed on both counts.

I wasn't sure how disillusioned *I* would be as the summer wore on. My comment to Hilary, a few nights before, had been accurate. I had never had any desire to be a mother and had reached thirty – well, twenty-nine if anyone asked – without ever having that view seriously challenged. Meeting a forty-two-year-old widower, with kids, a little over a year ago, had not made any difference. He couldn't father any more, to my relief, and both of his were normally safely ensconced in boarding school. I had met them, maybe half a dozen times, at weekends, and the few days we had all spent together at his place, at Christmas, had actually been fun. Christmas is a time for kids, but it was me who wasn't ready to grow up yet.

The small part of the responsible adult in me was trying to organize what my two brothers and I jokingly called a spare bedroom, when I heard the telephone ringing. This particular room was in the last of what had once been a terrace of three cottages, and probably the furthest from the current, now only, front door. I hadn't been in there for weeks, and couldn't, for a moment, remember where the nearest phone was. I scrambled out of the debris as it stopped ringing.

A voice shouted up the stairs: 'Ally, it's for you!'

'Coming!' I replied, and marched along a landing that hadn't been there six months ago. I found a telephone sitting on two bricks at the point where the landing ended at a hole in the wall. I heard Andy put the other phone down, somewhere in the house, as I answered.

'Hello?'

'Is that Alison Sheldon?'

'Yes, it is.'

'Oh, my name is Mrs McBain. I'm a friend of Mary Sanders.'

Inwardly I groaned. Mary Sanders was one of my aging, eternally grateful clients, who persisted in passing on my name to all and ancient sundry who wanted their loos decorated, or their tap washers replaced, or cat flaps installed, and welcomed the slightly uncommon concept of a woman builder to do the work. I listened with half an ear to the proposed job, while looking around pointlessly for pen and paper among the bricks. I had just managed to find a crumb of chalk and an off-cut of plasterboard on which to write, when I heard the comment I had come to expect from friends of Mary Sanders.

'It is unusual to have a woman in your line of work.'

'Well, my dad was a builder and my mum did all the decorating, so I suppose it runs in the family.'

I missed her next remark, while wondering how many times I had said that, this year alone. I wrote down her number and promised faithfully to phone later, when I had checked my appointments diary, to arrange a visit to view the proposed re-varnishing of her front door. When the doorbell rang, I arrived to open it still clutching my oversized notepad.

I was beaten to the door by Andy. Judging by his enthusiasm, I assumed he was awaiting someone else's arrival. *He* was disappointed, even if Derek's daughter wasn't.

Derek grinned at me. Tony galloped indoors uninvited and Sarah stopped, frozen to the spot at being confronted by my brother.

'Andy, you remember Sarah, don't you?' I said, trying to rescue the situation as tactfully as possible and remind him of her name.

'Of course,' he replied, gently taking her hand and kissing the back of it.

Derek and I exchanged amused glances, while his daughter visibly melted.

I walked out to the car with Derek, calling back to my brother to give us a hand. Andy, having stunned his young admirer, readily followed.

'You're a right sod,' I muttered to him, as he caught us up. 'You know she fancies you like mad!'

'She's got good taste,' he replied. 'Now, what's got to go in?'

We settled both children in their rooms. Sarah would be staying in the only spare room that actually resembled a bedroom. We put Tony in the semi-building site part of the house. To start with, he would most likely think it was cool, and it also gave us a chance, should time allow, to carry on with some work in the other bedroom.

Our decision was approved by Tony's 'Wow!' when he saw the large television perched on four boxes of floor tiles. 'Does it work?'

'Yes, it's all plugged in, ready to go, but don't have it on too loud because you'll wake up my big brother, Phil. His room's across the landing.'

'I won't, promise.'

We left him to sort himself out and probably turn on the television.

'Phil's new girlfriend has been staying for the last couple of weekends, so I doubt Tony will disturb him, whatever he does.'

'Is that the girl we met at that party?'

'Yes, she seems pleasant enough.'

'I thought she was nice. Let's hope it lasts.'

I gave Derek a sideways glance as we headed downstairs. 'I hope so too. He hasn't had much luck since the divorce, and he is a lovely guy.'

Derek gave me a hug. 'It is possible to find really good new partners, you know.'

I smiled up at him and we paused to give each other a quick kiss in the doorway of the lounge.

'Do you two mind?' Andy said from inside the room.

'Date let you down, has she?' I asked him, as I walked over to pour us a drink.

'No, she'll be here.'

'Do we know this one?' Before he had a chance to reply, I added, 'Mind you, do we know any of them?'

He treated me to a sarcastic smile. 'Oh well, if she's late I'll just have to seduce Derek's daughter.'

I noticed Derek's quick glance over his shoulder, to make sure Sarah was not in earshot before he joined in the banter. 'That'd take about thirty seconds,' he muttered.

I looked at my tall, skinny brother. 'Don't wind her up, Andy, she is only fifteen, and a very young fifteen!'

He would have replied, but Sarah walked into the room at that moment.

My gallant brother jumped to his feet. 'Have a chair,' he said, waving to the one he'd just vacated. 'And would you like a glass of wine? I'm sure your dad won't mind.'

I attempted to glare at him, but he refused to catch my eye. He was enjoying the adulation. Derek nodded reluctant approval to a small drink.

I looked from daughter to father. They were quite alike: tall, slim, both with fairly short, dark hair. Sarah was beginning to grow into a very attractive woman, but she didn't seem to be aware of it, which was rather nice. Derek had a kind face, which I'd noticed when we first met. He wasn't incredibly good-looking – like Rob had been – but he had a lovely smile and a gentleness about him that was very endearing. The whole family was quite sporty. Sarah was on school and club netball teams and played tennis to a good standard. Derek and I hammered the hell out of each other on the squash court most weeks.

He had been bearded when we'd met, but the new clean-shaven look had lopped years off him. No one realized he was twelve years my senior, and it didn't mean that much to either of us. With his bushy, blond beard, Phil probably looked older than Derek, and he was only thirty-three.

We were all fair-haired in our family. Andy wore his too long and was constantly having to brush it out of his eyes. Our mum had spent years moaning at him to have it cut, but he had always claimed that it added to his natural charm. As much as he drove me crazy sometimes, I had to admit that Andy never suffered from a shortage of female admirers.

My hair was short, naturally a bit spiky and normally did its own thing. It was a cause of constant annoyance when I was trying to get ready to go out. Both my brothers had an irritating habit of ruffling it, whenever I managed to get it to lie down; Derek had recently joined in the practice, which didn't make him quite so endearing. Tony had obviously noticed his dad doing this and decided to join in. He gave me a cheeky grin as he came into the lounge and made my already messy hair even more dishevelled.

'Get off!' I shouted, with a smile, as he ran away from me.

The doorbell rang again. There was no way that Andy was going to destroy his suave image in front of his admirer by rushing out of the room, so I successfully beat him to the front door. He followed fairly closely behind me, obviously annoyed that I had managed to get a glimpse of his date. When I opened the door I wished I hadn't. The tall, stunningly attractive ash-blonde, in a tight-fitting scarlet dress that revealed not a single unwanted ripple, glanced briefly across me, with a polite smile, then beamed a row of obscenely even, white teeth at my brother. Andy arrived, brushing his hair aside. She stepped back, aware that she was not about to come inside. My brother, with a dismissive 'Thank you, Alison,' as if he was talking to the maid, followed her out to her car – the latest 5-series BMW. I stood, for a moment, in my jeans, T-shirt and bare feet, and watched Andy open her door for her, alongside my mud-splattered, three-year-old estate car, filled with dust sheets, tools and lumps of timber.

Sarah looked a little less radiant when I returned to the lounge, and Tony had a protruding bottom lip, displaying a very distinct sulk. I raised an inquiring eye at Derek.

'Tony has suddenly gone off the idea of going out for a curry,' his father announced.

'I thought you liked curry,' I said to him.

Derek replied instead. 'There's football on the television.'

I looked round at all three of them and thought, God, this is going to be a long summer.

An hour later, compromise saw us tucking into a delivered takeaway, with the second half of the football being recorded, and no one allowed to disclose the result if heard by accident.

'Was this ever an *actual* farm?' Sarah suddenly asked.

'A long time ago it was. But the owners let it run down, when they died it was sold off in plots. These were just three farm-workers' cottages, but the plot included five acres of land.'

'Are you going to have animals?' Tony asked, through a crunch of poppadom.'

'Don't speak with your mouth full,' Derek muttered, out of habit.

'We have a house full of animals,' I answered, with feeling.

Sarah looked as if she was about to jump to my brother's defence at that remark, but then decided against it, especially as her own brother had found the comment funny.

'My parents bought it at a really stupid price, probably because it needed so much work done to it, but from a builder's point of view it was a snip, with tons of potential. We moved in, as a family, with ideas that stretched to the moon.'

'Are you all builders?' Sarah suddenly seemed to find the whole concept of builders fascinating, although I suspected it had more to do with finding out what Andy did.

'Apart from Phil. He's a PE teacher.'

'Even your mum?' Tony exclaimed.

'In a way. She was an interior designer – a very good one. She did all the decorating, and her ideas were magic.'

'What does Andy do?'

I tried to suppress the smile. 'What he *used* to do was plastering. That was what he was trained as, but these days I often wonder. Ask him, and all he'll reply is, "This and that". I guess you'd probably have to describe him as an entrepreneur. If people want things, he finds them. If people want workers, he arranges them. If someone wants something that no other person on earth can find, Andy will find it. I have no idea where his contacts come from, and I probably don't want to know, but he is useful to have around. He's also probably worth a fortune!'

Sarah looked very pleased with my reply. I felt a sudden desire to add that Andy was a complete sod, who'd never had one girlfriend for longer than six weeks, and that, more than once, we had had very irate fathers turning up on the doorstep, determined to thump him. I wanted to tell her that Andy's promises rarely meant what they said. But he was my brother. He'd never – to my knowledge – got any girl pregnant, and he'd never actually promised to marry anyone; they just got the wrong end of the stick. He was the ultimate free spirit, and it suited him, and a shy teenager, thirteen years his junior, was not going to be the one that tamed him.

Instead I went on, 'My parents died before we really got started on all the ideas we had for this place.'

That left me with a pang of sadness and my silence was uninterrupted, even by the kids. I glanced up and caught Derek looking at me. We smiled.

'It wasn't long after that that Phil got divorced. It just made sense for him to move back home, and for the three of us to tear the place to pieces and do what my parents originally intended. We might actually finish it, one day.'

'Did Andy already live here?' Sarah asked.

'Well, he certainly had a room here that was his. His things were in it, and he popped in to collect them once in a while. This was the address he wrote down. This was the phone number he gave out. So, in theory, I suppose he did.'

It should have been enough to put her off, but like most of the women who fell madly in love with my irresponsible kid brother, I think she thought that she could be the one that made a difference.

Yes, it was going to be a long summer.

Chapter 5

I was standing in the kitchen, less than half awake, waiting for the kettle to boil. Eight thirty on a Sunday morning was a time I very infrequently discovered existed at all, but I had forgotten that Derek's two were not normal kids. With body clocks still on boarding-school time, their attempts at quietly finding anything edible, or even tea or coffee, had finally made me despair of my attempts to go back to sleep. Some element of deep-seated idiocy had then offered them a cooked breakfast, and it seemed I had been preparing food and making endless drinks ever since.

The kitchen door opened and my elder brother shuffled inside. 'Hi,' he grunted at me, with a huge yawn. He was vaguely dressed, in tracksuit bottoms and an aging T-shirt that read: *Rugby players love a good ruck.* The fact that he had made an effort to find some clothes at all, rather than appear only in boxer shorts, at least proved he'd remembered we had guests, but he still seemed surprised, when he actually got his eyes in focus, at finding a kitchen full of people. Probably, like me, he believed that being up, dressed and fully awake at this time on a Sunday morning was inhuman.

'Tony, Sarah, this is my big brother, Phil.'

They both nodded a slightly shy greeting.

He gave them a sleepy smile and then noticed their dad. 'Hello, Derek, how are you doing?'

'Fine thanks, you?'

'Think so.' He pinched the boiled water from the kettle and slopped it into a mug of coffee.

'You on your own?' I asked.

'Nope,' he said, looking round for another mug to fill up, 'but Kath's got to go this afternoon. She's got some stuff she needs to do for the morning. Are we doing some work today?'

'That's what we said. Besides,' I added, smiling at the kids, 'we've got two more pairs of hands today.'

Tony grinned at me. Sarah, I noticed, was watching Phil. Tall and muscular, he looked every bit the rugby player that he was. Piercing blue eyes shone out from the slightly unkempt hairy framework. I wondered if her adulation was switching brothers. With that thought, the younger version appeared in the doorway.

'Just getting up or just getting home?' Phil inquired.

Andy pulled a sarcastic smile and turned to walk back out of the kitchen.

'Richard!' Phil called after him.

'What?' Andy's voice floated back.

'We said we'd work today.'

'I know.'

Tony looked from my brother to me with a confused frown. 'Why did he call him Richard?'

Phil and I gave the well-practised reply, ''Cos he's a right dick!' Then we both grinned in momentary guilt that perhaps it was not the place for that standard answer – to an eleven-year-old. Said eleven-year-old giggled, predictably.

Our established views on when a day's work should start, on a Sunday, were not quite in tune with two very early-rising youngsters. Tony's eagerness to help was probably more to do with a chance to get really dirty than do anything approaching work. Our idea of work, however, was not his. We worked on the house most Sunday afternoons, for about four hours, and we all did our best to find a few days whenever Phil was on school holidays. He broke up later than Derek's kids, so that piece of scheduling had not yet even been considered. It was little wonder that the house changed extremely slowly.

I'd probably been aware, had I chosen to really notice, that Tony was getting bored at the inactivity that was evident throughout the household. By the time Phil had reappeared, fully dressed, and Andy had returned from at least half an hour in the bathroom with the Sunday papers, and Kath had joined us and been introduced, and everyone had had yet more tea or coffee, Tony had given up the impatient wriggling around in his chair and had vanished into the garden. Sarah looked uncomfortable too. Part of it was maybe that boarding-school routine didn't allow for long, lazy mornings, but in Sarah's case it probably had more to do with an urge – tempered by a shy inability – to start a conversation with Andy. He didn't believe Sundays started until he'd consumed his first beer for lunch, and anyway, to him – and, I have to admit, to me as well – mornings were definitely *not* a time for conversation.

I could recognize in Derek the calm enjoyment of having a little bit of the responsibility of both his children removed from him. They were only with him during school holidays, and some weekends, but even that, I knew, he found draining, with two bundles of endless energy simultaneously demanding attention.

When Phil inquired if we were going to the pub, Sarah lapsed into despair and followed her younger brother outside. Their reappearance a few minutes later woke everyone from gentle inactivity, as they crashed into the kitchen, both talking excitedly.

'Whoa, slow down,' Derek reprimanded them. 'What the hell's the matter?'

'There's two foxes in the garden!' they replied in unison.

Momentarily shocked at their sudden entrance and fearful of some disaster, we all relaxed again.

'Oh,' Andy said, and picked up the sports section again.

I smiled at them. 'We get loads of wildlife out here. You might even see them feeding near the house tonight.'

'Yeah?' Tony looked amazed. 'Really close to the house?'

'The ultimate waste disposal unit,' Phil commented.

'I expect they were there last night, but we weren't looking,' I told them. 'We always put food out, and all the scraps. We get badgers as well.'

'Would they come if we put food out now?'

'No, you'll have to wait until it's dark, or at least getting dark.'

'Unless Sam comes back,' Andy mumbled from behind the paper.

'Who's Sam?' Sarah asked, clearly happy to have an excuse to speak to him. She was rewarded with the paper being put down.

'She was a vixen that used to come and demand food, morning and afternoon, in broad daylight. She would actually take it from your hand. We christened her Sam.' He shrugged at two blank faces and returned to his reading.

'Sadly, she hasn't been for months,' I went on, 'but you never know, she's reappeared before, after an age.'

Phil got to his feet and wrapped his arms round Kath's neck. 'Time for a quick pint before you go?'

'Yes, I think so.'

'Okay, see you lot there,' he said, and the two ambled from the room.

'Lunch in a pub?' Sarah asked, her voice echoing the look of boredom on her brother's face at having to sit around even longer before they could do anything.

'Not lunch, just a drink, to get us in the mood for working. We'll have a sandwich, or something, during the afternoon.'

'Would you like to come in my car?' Andy asked her, bundling up the newspaper.

Boredom vanished.

*

By about five thirty that afternoon both youngsters were beginning to see the benefits of lazy mornings. We didn't always work quite as manically as that day, but having two extra, young and enthusiastic helpers seemed too good an opportunity to pass up. We had set ourselves a target for totally clearing all the rubbish out of one of the bedrooms. That included demolishing an old built-in cupboard and ripping off skirtings and architrave. Tony thought it was wonderful, and as most of it could be burned, we had the kids running up and down the stairs, to and from a huge bonfire raging in the barren bit of garden we used for that purpose. I found it quite a relief, by then, that they looked exhausted. I did a manual job most days, but to me this was pretty boring, as well as being a busman's holiday, and although it was good to finally be able to see the shape of the bedroom, I had had enough.

We all stood around, staring at the diminishing bonfire, drinking various things from cans. At last Phil broke the trance. 'How many for dinner?'
Both youngsters exchanged bemused glances as initially no one answered what appeared to be a straightforward question, and then, as the silence grew longer, both my brothers and I started to grin. The grins turned to audible chuckles, and Andy, with a vaguely impolite retort, turned round and headed for the house.

'We take it in turns to cook on Sundays,' I explained to their curious expressions. 'It's become a bit of a ritual, so one day a week we can sit down and eat together. Otherwise, we just seem to pass on the stairs and never catch up with each other. It's also, usually, the one day we don't have guests. I suppose it's our "family evening", but Andy prefers two of the weeks to the other one. Cooking's not his favourite pastime.'

'Will he cook for all of us?' Derek asked.

Phil nodded. 'That's why it's funny,' he said, then shouted after Andy, 'Bring back a few more beers!'

The response was a gesture rather than words.

*

We sat down to eat at gone eight. That was quite normal for us, but I think, by then, the kids were starving. Tony had already demolished two packets of crisps and half a packet of biscuits. Sarah had seemed to be attempting to play the adult role, and simply wait, but she had succumbed to a couple of biscuits. We, of course, were enjoying a few drinks before dinner, but I don't think she found the same pleasure in orange juice.

Andy had disappeared, with his normal, relaxed attitude, into the kitchen, ten or fifteen minutes before announcing dinner was ready. He may have appeared laid back as he ambled from the lounge, but I imagined the state of the kitchen told a rather different story.

The huge spread of roast lamb, mint sauce and a wide variety of vegetables impressed both Phil and me, but the kids appeared to take it in their stride. I supposed that they always had food put in front of them, either at school or by their dad. To them it wasn't so surprising that a young, single gadabout could produce something like this.

We had barely finished eating when the phone rang. Phil was nearest and answered.

'Ally, it's Kris.'

'Oh, right.'

As I got up, Derek explained to the kids, 'Kris plays in Ally's band.'

I felt a distinct twang of annoyance, and suppressed a momentary urge to snap at him, You don't know *all* my friends!

A few minutes later I returned to the table. 'We need to have our practice Tuesday, instead of Wednesday,' I told Derek. 'We hadn't arranged anything, had we?'

He shook his head. 'Maybe we could come and listen?' he suggested.

I sensed an instant excitement in both the kids.

'No one listens to our rehearsals,' I replied at once, reaching for the wine bottle to top up my glass, so I didn't have to look at any of them. Alongside me, I was aware that Tony's head had dropped in disappointment. My gaze flickered across Andy's face as I put the bottle down. He gave me an almost imperceptible nod of approval. *You* would agree, wouldn't you? I thought to myself. My brother kept the different aspects of his life in very carefully separated compartments. He believed it saved him unnecessary hassle and unwanted questions. Perhaps we were more alike than I had realized.

I buried the twinge of guilt and decided to soften the blow a little. 'We're playing a gig at a barn dance in a couple of weeks,' I told them, 'and I hope everyone's going to come to that.'

'Are you playing for the dancing?'

'No, we're doing a half-hour set in the interval, then rounding the evening off with another set.' I smiled. 'How long that lasts will depend on how much they like us.'

'Or how much they hate barn dancing,' Andy added.

The phone rang again and I hoped it might be Hilary. Sadly, it was for Andy, and we didn't see him again for twenty minutes.

Chapter 6

Tony was struggling to stay awake, but he was determined to see the foxes. He was rewarded with the arrival of three boisterous, fairly young cubs.

'Wow! Cool!'

Even Sarah was fascinated. 'They keep looking in here, but they don't seem to worry about us at all.'

'They'd probably go if you stood up, but while we don't move much, they'll just carry on feeding.'

Derek glanced across at me. I think he was as absorbed with the wildlife display as his children.

'Have you ever photographed any of this?'

'Not very successfully. Enough to see what's there, but I think we'd probably need a special sort of film to do it justice.'

'You should try. It'd be great. Can I get my camera and give it a go?'

'No, don't!' Sarah exclaimed. 'If you move, they'll run off.'

'They'll run off if the badger comes,' Phil told them. He had joined us, but Andy had vanished somewhere, to Sarah's evident disappointment. She kept glancing at the door, in case he appeared.

'What else comes?' Tony asked.

'Oh, all sorts of things. Pheasants, quite often, until they become someone's dinner, hedgehogs, loads of bloody squirrels. We've seen stoats and weasels, and the odd grass snake.'

The kids shivered.

'And deer.' Phil grinned.

'But no aardvarks,' I replied, laughing.

I glanced round at three puzzled faces.

'A few weeks ago, we had a stag turn up in the garden. We've seen deer nearby on the odd occasion, but never close to the house before. A friend of Andy's was staying, and she'd got up to go to the loo.'

'It was about half five in the morning,' Phil added.

I nodded. 'She saw the stag and woke Andy up to tell him. He then woke both of us up, so we didn't miss it.'

Phil carried on. 'So there's the four of us, at this ungodly hour on a Sunday morning, in some pretty strange nightwear, standing staring into the garden.'

'After that,' I explained, 'we made a rule that no one was to wake anyone up in the middle of the night to see animals in the garden, unless there was an aardvark.'

'Could one turn up?' Tony asked, eagerly.

We all laughed, and I felt sorry for him. He looked embarrassed.

'No,' I said, squeezing his shoulder, 'they only live in Africa.'

'Perhaps one will escape from the zoo,' he suggested, trying to put right his mistake.

'You never know.'

We all sat for a few moments, watching the foxes clear all the scraps outside.

'Are we going away on holiday?' Sarah asked suddenly.

Tony, who had been trying not to let anyone see he was yawning, instantly woke up. 'Yeah, Dad, are we?'

This, I decided instantly, was nothing to do with me. Derek may have made some vague suggestion about us all going away, but I really hoped he'd forgotten that, so I got up to pour another drink and left it to Dad to sort out.

'Well,' he replied, 'no one's told me what they want to do yet.'

Both kids started talking at once.

'Hold on,' Derek said firmly, with both hands in the air. 'First, I do have to do some work, so I can't have more than the odd day off for a week or so. Second, you said you want to go to football camp, at some time, Tony, but you haven't told me when it is. And third, Sarah, you said you've been invited to go to Dorset for a week with your friend and her parents, but I don't know when that's supposed to be either.'

He was instantly bombarded with an assortment of dates and wild suggestions for holidays, with both kids trying to talk over each other. Through the noise, I was very aware that both had said, in their own ways, that their pre-arranged trips didn't matter a bit if they were all going to go away together.

I felt a slight lump in my throat at the closeness of them all. I loved both my brothers dearly – we could never have lived together if we didn't get on extremely well – but this was a family unity that I don't think I had ever known. In a strange way, I was a little envious.

'Okay, that's sorted then,' Derek said, although as far as I could tell nothing had been sorted, and I doubt he had been able to hear either of them or understand anything through the cacophony. 'I will make the decision, and you two will just have to put up with it!'

Both of them were grinning broadly. I wondered if this was some strange summer holiday ritual that they always went through. What was clear was that neither of the kids cared where they went or what they did, as long as they were all on holiday together. There was something special about it. Maybe it was because they no longer had a mother, or maybe it was simply because Derek was a special kind of father. I suddenly became aware that Phil was looking at me. I caught his eye and we smiled at each other. Maybe we had both observed the closeness, or, more likely, he recognized that I was definitely staying out of the conversation.

The next remark totally caught me off guard.

'Will you come with us, Ally?'

The question came from Sarah. This time I didn't have to look at Phil to know he had just held his breath. I might have expected a tentative inquiry from Derek, in private, but not from his daughter.

'This is *your* holiday,' I said carefully. 'The *three of you.*'

'It'd be cool if you came,' Tony added enthusiastically.

'Oh, you're not going somewhere hot, then?' I responded flippantly, and instantly regretted it when I saw his hopeful smile. 'Seriously, though, you three need to be together. Family trips are important.'

'We would all love you to come with us,' Derek said.

I was beginning to feel trapped.

'I don't manage to have summer holidays,' I said. 'I never do. Most of my clients know I'm a skiing freak and go away in the winter – that's why I get so booked up in the summer. Also, we need to do some work on the house.' As I added the last bit, I hoped that Phil would not ruin things by saying it wasn't a problem, but, *bless him,* he kept quiet.

I could see by the three expectant faces that my struggling excuses were getting me nowhere. 'I'm starting a new job tomorrow, and I've got at least four scheduled in after that. The guys that work for me depend on it too.'

'So, leave Mark in charge,' Derek suggested.

I came close to snapping. In my head, I screamed, You can't talk about Mark, you don't know anything about him! Instead I replied, 'And I've got a gig in a fortnight.'

'We can go the day after,' Tony said, cheerfully. 'We've got eight weeks.'

'I'll have to look at my diary,' I finished, rather lamely. 'But I'm not promising anything.'

From the looks on the two young faces in front of me, I felt like I just had.

Derek, it seemed, was going to be as persistent as his children, although his suggestion was less frightening. 'Perhaps we could manage just a few days, all four of us, on a boat maybe.'

'A boat? Oh, cool!'

'What, *staying* on a boat?' Sarah asked.

'Yes, on the river, or one of the canals,' Derek replied.

Both kids suddenly looked as if all their Christmases had come at once. I looked across at Derek. 'I'll check the work situation tomorrow and see if it's possible, but the gig has to come first.' I had a feeling that I'd just been expertly manipulated.

I went out to make some coffee and Derek bullied both the children to go to bed. Tony put his head round the kitchen door on his way past.

'Will you call me if the aardvark comes?' he said.

'You'll be the first person I tell.'

He responded with a broad smile from a sleepy face that had fought tiredness for a bit too long, then he turned and plodded off up the stairs.

Phil took his coffee and disappeared.

Derek watched him go. 'Did he do that to leave us alone?'

'No. If you want to be on your own with someone in this place, you're the one who has to move. I guess he just wanted some time to himself.'

Derek sipped the brandy Phil had poured for him. 'The kids like it here,' he said.

I felt a further stirring of apprehension. 'Sarah would like a garden shed, if Andy was in it.' I grinned, trying to keep it light.

He smiled back. 'I meant that the kids get on well with you.'

'They're nice kids,' I answered, struggling to find a means of easing away from this conversation. 'Not that I have any real experience with kids. Phil's better at all that; after all, he teaches them every day. I couldn't do his job if my life depended on it.'

'Neither could I, two's enough.'

'And only in small doses,' I added, thinking he could take that to mean whatever he liked.

He nodded. 'Very true.'

Maybe it hadn't been a discussion leading anywhere. Maybe I was just being oversensitive. Nevertheless, I didn't want that kind of conversation at all. Life was okay the way it was, and it didn't include any responsibility on my part towards Derek's offspring. I briefly imagined worrying about two kids falling off a boat, and wiped the thought away. It wasn't my scene at all.

I found myself wondering just how much I felt towards Derek. I liked him a lot. We got on easily, without effort, and normally had a good few laughs. I was very aware, however, that our time together never constituted a huge part of the week. We played squash on a Monday night, and usually had a meal afterwards, and we went out most Saturdays. That might – on the odd occasion – be for the whole day, but more often it was just the evening, and then we would stay at his place or mine. We parted around lunchtime on Sundays, so I could get on with work at home or sort out the following week. I realized that I had probably never even mentioned before that my Sunday evenings with my brothers were all but sacrosanct.

I did tell him about the other things I did. He knew all about the band, knew that I had regular evenings out with Hilary, and that I went to keep fit most Thursday nights. He was aware that I made a point of meeting up with my friends as often as I could. I told him about my evenings out, but he wasn't included.

He lived about an hour and a half's drive away, and his computer consultancy work kept him pretty busy. He worked long, and often odd, hours. He wasn't included in the rest of my life because circumstances made it impossible. Suddenly he was here, though, and it *would* be possible. It made me start to look at things differently. I wasn't sure I wanted him in the rest of my life.

It was then I realized he had asked me something.

'What? Sorry, I was daydreaming about work.'

'Are we going to play squash tomorrow?'

'What about the kids?'

'I suppose they could come and watch.'

'That's not very exciting. Why don't you take them for a game? You're not working tomorrow, are you? You could probably book a double slot earlier in the day. I'm starting a new job, so I'll probably be back a bit later than usual.'

I was starting to build my defences.

Chapter 7

It was Tuesday, and I was aware of a little black cloud sitting over my head as I woke up. I had agreed to take Sarah to work with me this morning. Tony was going with Derek, who had to set up a system, for a couple of hours. I think that's what he said, anyway. I wasn't really listening. Tony was fascinated by anything to do with computers, so he would happily watch what was going on and ask endless questions. To Sarah, and to me, they were simply a tool to use; neither of us had any urge to delve into their make-up or find out how they worked. That was why, in a moment of weakness, I had said she could come with me. My black cloud was worsened by Derek saying that when he and Tony had finished they would go off to find some holiday brochures and meet us for lunch.

Mark and I had started our pensioner's bedroom the day before, and I had left him to finish it today, with Les, one of my occasional workmen. Les was actually retired, and an excellent decorator. He welcomed the chance to escape from home, now and then, and do a couple of days' work.

I had opted to answer a call from a regular client, who I knew would have no problem with me bringing along an observer. It was going to be a quick job, giving us the option of meeting the others for lunch, after which I could get rid of Sarah, back to her dad, then check in on Mark and Les. Sarah had given her dad a broad smile as we left the house when I mentioned she was about to be a plumber's mate.

The client's toilet cistern was overflowing, and while I was there, they asked if I could change four tap washers, before the dripping drove them mad. I knew this house backwards; I was in there at least three times a year. It wasn't always for plumbing, by any means – in fact, they refused to have any work done by anyone else – but, nevertheless, I could still have crawled across their loft and turned off both gate valves in the dark.

I did turn the loft light on, however, to show Sarah what a gate valve was, and do a brief explanation on supply pipes for hot and cold water. That was where the cockiness – and the luck – came to an end. The valve to shut off the cold supply was absolutely stuck fast. I hate trying to shift gate valves or stopcocks with wrenches because they can break so easily. The image I had been carefully cultivating – master tradesperson, calm, collected and totally in control – disappeared with the first 'Oh, shit!' and I began to have visions of flooded lofts, insurance claims and the like.

With a bit of inward panic, I finally managed to shift the offending gate valve, and heard the encouraging sound of slowing water from the tap below me in the bathroom. It refused to close completely, but I could live with the remaining trickle. The hot water valve turned instantly and, with renewed self-assurance, I climbed down from the loft, explaining to Sarah that the hot water would take a fraction longer to slow down, owing to the supply being cut off to the bottom of the cylinder, and the hot coming out of the top, and the amount in the pipes…until it was clear she had lost interest. By that time, the tap should have dripped dry, but steaming water was still gushing forth with the same gusto. My credibility took a further nosedive, but I quickly spotted a way to restore it, in the form of a stopcock, low down on the cylinder supply pipe. That, however, proved to be beyond even my largest adjustable spanner.

By the time I had turned off the mains supply to the tank and drained it, both Sarah, who was now wishing she'd spent a boring morning in the office with her father, and the client, who had, without thinking, flushed the last cistern-full of water in the toilet, were getting a little restless.

At last I ended up with an empty tank, empty cistern and four dry taps, and commenced a job that should have started some half-hour previously. Renewing the ball valve on the toilet was easy, restoring my street credibility and briefly interesting Sarah, but after such a start four straightforward washers were too much to hope for. Three were textbook. The fourth had been fitted – probably some time during the First World War – with a brittle plastic washer, which jammed inside the tap housing and broke into six pieces as I bad-temperedly heaved out the assembly. Four of the six pieces dropped back down the pipe.

For Sarah it was most enjoyable part of the day. Turning the mains water back on to refill the tank, without the top on the tap, seemed to Sarah to be slightly cranky. As the water started to appear, I waited hopefully for the washer fragments to emerge with the flow. I could see them, tantalizingly close, but the water wasn't strong enough. I clamped a thumb over the top and told her to turn off the bath taps. I removed my thumb. The water hit me straight in the face. I was pleased to see bits of washer gush forth. Sarah was almost hysterical. I was beginning to have trouble keeping the cheerful smile, as she had been supposed to run to the kitchen and turn off the mains supply, instead of laughing at me getting wet, but at least now I was almost finished with the tap washers and I could fill the tank.

Sarah quickly returned to being completely bored, but the client was happy enough. She could now refill the kettle, having used its contents as a poor substitute for flushing the loo. She made tea for all of us and got me to agree to decorate the spare bedroom some time in the next few weeks. Quite where I was going to find the time was beyond even my greatest piece of imaginative planning.

As we left the house, I found that Sarah was a totally useless substitute for Mark. Walking towards the car, she jumped as I suddenly broke the silence. '*No!*' I snapped. Then I spoke again, with less aggression, 'Um, no, I'm afraid not.'

By now Sarah was looking sideways at me, as if I had completely lost the plot.

'I would love to, but right now it's just impossible,' I said, then changed it to, 'As soon as I have a space, I will phone and let you know.'

Eventually, Sarah asked, 'What *are* you talking about?'

'I'm practising,' I answered. 'One of these days I'll learn how to say no when a client wants a job done that's completely out of the question, instead of trying to make them feel that I can do something I can't.'

'Oh' she said, quietly.

For a moment I believed that was the end of the conversation; then she went on, 'Is that what you were doing on Sunday, when I asked if you'd come away with us?'

I stopped dead in my tracks and stared at her. This was one perceptive teenager, which was something I needed like a hole in the head right now.

'Clients are my livelihood,' I said slowly. 'I can't afford to be totally honest with them about things like that. I can't afford to say that I can't do anything for six months, which is probably nearer the truth. These people always use me, and I depend on that for a regular income. If I tell them how long they might actually have to wait, they'll find someone else. The six months will come to an end, and then what happens if all my clients have gone elsewhere?'

'So you'll just keep putting them off?'

I was having trouble keeping my temper. I didn't need a philosophical fifteen-year-old having a go at me right now.

'No,' I replied, through slightly gritted teeth, 'I will do what they ask. I will find the time, even if that means working late nights and weekends. I will put up with the emotional and physical stress that causes, I will smile at them all the way through the job, and at the end of it say, "You're welcome!"' I took a huge inward breath and puffed it out with an angry shake of the head. It was probably the most truthful I had been in years about how self-destructive I was in running my business. Deep down, I knew I needed to be needed, and bending over backwards to accommodate clients, who thought I was wonderful, was the best way I knew to achieve that. What I *didn't* need was some child forcing me to admit it! Mark and I would have simply laughed about it together, and then practised a hundred ways of saying no.

Sarah remained perceptive enough to say no more. In fact she said nothing until we were almost at the restaurant where we were meeting Derek and Tony for lunch. We were nearly an hour late.

'Can I tell them how to change tap washers?' she asked, as, miraculously, I found a parking space right outside.

This fifteen-year-old, I decided, must have been born at least fifty years ago.

As we sat down I listened to Sarah's amusing – although I have to say, embellished – account of the morning's work. She had a very sharp-witted way of describing events. The entire conversation was at my expense, but I felt no animosity towards me from her monologue. That was an art that defied people way beyond her years. This was a very intelligent, and genuine, youngster, who had a much greater depth of understanding than I had realized.

Tony was less entertained than Derek and I were. He was too eager to recount his own morning. He, at least, was what one expected of a kid his age.

'We found a boat!' he announced, as soon as he could grab a moment to speak. 'It's really cool. It's white, with loads of rooms, and you sit right up on top to steer it. Dad's asked them to hold it till tomorrow. It's even got a television!'

I felt an instant flare-up of mixed emotions again. Now I *was* trapped.

Chapter 8

The small black cloud I had woken up to the previous morning had grown to storm-force today. Hilary would probably have laughed until she cried – I was taking both kids to work with me! As a last resort for preserving my sanity, I made a mental note to phone Hilary during the morning and tell her what I was doing. Perhaps mild hysterics down the phone would rub off a bit.

Mark had been quite happy about having them in the house while we were working. I wondered if his growing obsession with the actress was bringing out his broody side…

Mark and Les were already there when we arrived. I was not in the best of moods, as both kids had taken ages to make up their minds what to wear. Derek, who wasn't leaving until later, had been no help, just telling them both to ask me. My repeated comments of, 'You're going to get dirty,' had apparently not helped either. Tony had been unable to choose between looking like a cricketer, in whites, which he thought might be the right thing for painting, or resembling a lumberjack, in checked shirt and his heaviest boots. He finally settled for an opening batsman. Sarah seemed only to want to look her best in what she believed was her scruffiest gear. The final choice was more akin to what I would have worn out on a Saturday night. Maybe at fifteen I would have taken hours over what to wear when I was meeting new people – particularly men. This morning, I didn't feel I could even remember that far back.

Les opened the door to us, which I found mildly amusing, as Sarah obviously wasn't expecting to meet anyone quite so ancient.

'With or without sugar?' a voice yelled from inside.

'Both without!' I shouted back.

We followed the sound of the voice and I opened my mouth to introduce the kids to Mark. I didn't even get a word out before he had shot across the room, grabbed me in his arms and swung me round.

'She got the part!'

'Brilliant!' was my muffled reply, my head buried somewhere in his shoulder.

Finally he put me down and I succeeded in telling everyone who everyone else was.

It took a few moments to realize that both the kids seemed wary of Mark. Perhaps wary was too conservative a word. Tony seemed to be more shy than ever, and Sarah looked positively sulky. I barely had time to register their facial expressions, before Mark came and put an arm around me. I flopped my head onto his shoulder, as I often did.

'I feel like celebrating,' he announced.

'That's the best offer you've had all day,' Les commented, from the doorway.

'It's the *only* offer,' I replied, and the three of us laughed.

Les shook his head. 'You two want your heads bashing together,' he muttered as he wandered from the room.

Mark gave me a squeeze and a kiss on the cheek and went to retrieve his mug of tea.

'Right, you guys, who's painting and who's pasting?'

Two young faces stared at him without a word. I took in all the expressions, and lack of communication, and opted for escape.

'Mark's in charge this morning,' I said, trying to suppress a smirk. 'He'll sort out what you're doing. I need to make a phone call and then shoot down the road for some paint.'

I left the kitchen and pulled a face at Les, who was hanging out of the front door, having a cigarette. 'Can I have one?' I pleaded.

He tossed over the packet. 'One of these days I *will* bash your heads together,' he commented.

I looked up at him, quizzically, as I accepted a light. He smiled at me, with a caring expression.

'You know you mean more to each other than anyone else in the world. Why the hell you don't both accept the fact, I'll never know.'

'It would never work,' I replied.

'Why not?'

'We're friends. We know each other too well.'

'And friends can't be lovers?'

I started to answer, but he cut me short.

'And I know you've been that as well!'

'You know too much!' I said, with a mock glare.

He shook his head gently. 'I've watched the pair of you, over the years, and if I didn't know better, I would think you were the happiest and the most suited couple I'd ever met.'

I shrugged. 'Right now Mark's besotted with the stage, anyway.'

'Are you certain about that?'

I looked up at him. 'You saw him, when I arrived. It was all he could talk about.'

'Well, it gave him an excuse to give you a hug.'

I laughed. 'He doesn't need an excuse.'

'*Exactly*,' Les answered. 'And you're out here escaping from the offspring of your latest boyfriend, because you don't really want them in your life. That's if you even want their father,' he added quietly.

I stared at him for some time, trying to conjure up a suitable reply and trying not to dwell on what he'd just said. Eventually I asked him, 'When did you take up psychology?'

'If one lives long enough,' he said, adeptly flicking his cigarette end into the open dustbin, 'one sees a lot of wasted lives. Old people have a chance to tell the young where they're going wrong, but the young know it all, so they don't listen.' He started to walk back into the house, then turned and smiled at me. 'Being old doesn't make us past it; it just gives us more experience.'

I watched until he disappeared from sight, then pulled my mobile phone from my belt and dialled.

'Hilary, it's me!'

*

I had managed, with some effort, to dismiss Les's comments from my mind, by the time I got back with the paint we needed. It hadn't been a conversation on which I wanted to reflect. I had talked myself into believing that his life was not too great, so he needed to sort out other people's to make himself feel better. However, that hadn't stopped me quoting it, verbatim, to Hilary. She had only made it worse by commenting, 'Is that news to you?' It was then I decided that the signal on my mobile was breaking up.

The front door was open. I was just about to shout that I was putting the kettle on, when I heard a young female voice saying, 'No, our mum's dead.' Feeling a little guilty, I walked quietly to the door of the room they were working in, and listened.

'Oh, I'm sorry. What happened?' Mark asked.

'Not sure,' Tony replied. 'We think she killed herself, though Dad said it was an accident.'

I felt a momentary pang of guilt at not having prepared Mark for this. I was about to walk into the room and try to put an end to the conversation, without letting on that I'd been eavesdropping, when Sarah took up the story.

'She had some sort of breakdown,' she said.

'She was a teacher,' Tony added. 'She used to be great helping with our homework. Then she just stopped doing it.'

I carried on listening.

'We used to come home and find her sitting doing nothing,' Sarah went on. 'No food for us, just nothing. Dad said she was ill and we needed to treat her gently, but she hardly even spoke to us.'

'Grandma and Grandpa used to come sometimes to look after us,' Tony said.

'*Huh!*'

I heard the venom in Sarah's voice.

'If *they* ever came, she was far worse afterwards! Grandfather just used to shout at her to pull herself together.'

'At least we got fed...' Tony said wistfully.

I allowed myself a small smile at the things that were important to a young lad.

'Couldn't the doctors help?' Mark asked.

'They sent her to see all sorts of people. They even put her in hospital a couple of times. She'd seem better and come home, and then it happened all over again. One day she just didn't come home.'

'It must have been really tough.'

'Oh, we were in boarding school by then. Dad didn't know what else to do. He had to keep working. Somebody had to.'

I reflected, sadly, on how much these kids had had to cope with, and also how – apparently – they accepted and understood it all. Maybe one day it would catch up with them. I hoped not. I began to realize just how much Derek meant to them, and, perhaps, why the holiday was so important. It didn't matter where they went, as long as they were together. God knows when the last real family holiday was, with their mother healthy. My fears returned with a vengeance. I was *not* about to become their substitute mother, under *any* circumstances!

Les suddenly appeared, catching me at the door. My shocked gasp was masked by him slamming the front door and shouting, 'Hi, Ally, got the paint?'

I looked at him with a mixture of guilt and gratitude, as I hastily walked back to the front door to answer, 'Yes, I've got it all. How's everything going?'

When I walked into the room it was obvious I had got away with my subterfuge. It appeared that it was their turn to pretend they'd been doing something else. They did look as if they were working; however, there was an evident lack of progress. Tony was struggling to paste a length of wallpaper and Sarah was scraping the last bits of old paper from the wall where a radiator had been. It was a great relief to me that the new wallpaper was only woodchip, as someone else would have to re-paste all Tony's edges before it was painted. He finally reached the end of the length and attempted to fold it, in the way I assumed Mark had shown him. He tore one corner and looked up guiltily.

'Don't worry, we can get over that. Ally will probably sack you, but I'm not that mean.'

They both smiled. They didn't seem so guarded with Mark now. I wondered how he'd managed to bring them round.

'I don't fire people for one mistake; I just send them to make the tea. *Now!*'

Tony jumped up with a grin and left the room.

I turned to Sarah. 'Can you check what Les wants and give Tony a hand?'

'You haven't scared them off, then?' I said in an undertone, very much aware that I could be heard outside the room.

'Actually, I did my very best to scare them. I didn't think they were going to speak to me at all, so I told them the tale of the hidden cellar.'

'With much embellishment, no doubt!'

'Of course. One creaking step at a time, through the cobwebs of ages, with a fading torch…and then what did we see? *Old bones!*'

I shook my head in amusement. 'Yeah, the skeletons of four dead rats.'

'It's a good story, though. Let's face it, it frightened us a bit before we ventured down those stairs. I seem to remember we were quite disappointed that no one had buried a body down there.'

'And I remember that you told the owners we'd just found Lord Lucan!'

He grinned. 'Anyway, after that Tony didn't seem to think I was all bad, so I started asking him what he was doing at school; then Sarah joined in, and then I asked about their family. Mind you, that might have been a mistake. They were just telling me about their mother when you came back.'

I nodded. 'I'm sorry, I should have warned you.'

Our conversation was curtailed by the appearance of the tea. Both kids sat on the floor, but they had fallen silent again. Mark decided that his original strategy worked best.

'Did I tell you about the day we found a hand grenade…?'

*

After lunch, with some trepidation, I let them loose with paint. This job consisted of a quick decoration of two rooms. The first had needed the woodchip; the second, where Les had already done the ceiling, just needed the walls painting. We left Mark to complete the papering, without the hindrance of assistance. He could now get on three times as fast, and Les could help him. Next door I spread out as many extra dust sheets as I possessed and showed them how to use a paint roller.

I was just concluding that I must possess a streak of insanity, and feeling thankful that everything would get a second coat, when my mobile rang. It was Derek. I told him that both kids had more paint on themselves than on the walls, but otherwise things were fine. Tony grinned at me. I finished the call and let them know that their dad was leaving work to go and book the boat. Tony's grin got bigger. My feelings of panic got bigger still.

Chapter 9

I was definitely not sorry when the day came to an end. As helpers, the kids had been quite a handicap. Fortunately it was only one day; Derek wasn't working in the morning. He could sort them out tomorrow, and my job should still finish on time, despite their 'assistance'.

At least I didn't lose my temper with them, I thought to myself, as we climbed into my car to go home. Sarah's first comment nearly changed that.

'You and Mark are very good friends, aren't you?'

'Yes, we are,' I replied, deliberately choosing not to justify the friendship in any way.

'Has Dad met him?'

I inwardly counted to about a hundred and ten, while studiously staring at the oncoming traffic. Finally, as I pulled out, I said, 'He has, once.'

'You seem to get on better with him than you do with Dad.'

I took a deep breath. I couldn't decide if it was concern for her father, fear of being abandoned by someone else in their lives or simply curiosity. Whichever it was, it was probably quite a brave remark on her part. I managed to find some more traffic that appeared to require my concentration, while I considered a response. In that moment I registered that Derek and I never got close to each other in their company; we never even held hands walking along, so Mark's display of affection would have given them a very different view of me.

'I've known Mark a great deal longer,' I answered, at last.

'I just wondered why you hadn't got together.'

'Sarah,' I said, as cheerfully as I could, 'that is absolutely none of your business.'

After a pause, she muttered, 'Sorry.'

It made for a rather silent journey home. We pulled into the drive and I noticed Andy's car. I hoped he was staying in for a while. It would distract Sarah, anyway.

I opened the door and shouted, 'Hi!' A response came from somewhere.

'We'd better go and change,' Sarah announced. 'Come on, Tony.'

That made me smile. Still in my work gear, I headed towards the drinks cabinet. The telephone rang as I was level with it. Assuming it was for Andy, I snatched it up, just to annoy him.

'May I speak to Alison Sheldon, please?'

I groaned inwardly. The last thing I needed right now was someone else wanting an urgent repair job done.

'Speaking.'

'This is Sister Kathy Mason, from A&E at St Joseph's hospital.'

I had a brief vision of redecorating an emergency department, but my thoughts were cut short.

'Derek Lee asked if I could contact you.'

My stomach flipped over in anticipation of the next part of the sentence. It came.

'He's been involved in a car accident…'

My mind reeled and I totally missed what she said next.

'I'm sorry, what did you say?'

'He is all right,' she repeated, slowly, 'but he has a broken leg, and he is a bit cut around the face.'

The built-in panic-merchant in me took over momentarily. How much was *a bit* to them? I tried to concentrate on her voice and make sense of what she was saying.

'…so if you could bring in some overnight things for him.'

'How many nights?' I gabbled, and then realized how daft that sounded. 'I'm sorry. It's a bit of a shock.' I was 'a bit' shocked'; Derek was 'a bit' cut. I hoped they didn't equate in terms of magnitude, because I was all too well aware of how dismayed I felt.

'Don't worry, he's quite comfortable. I'll tell him you'll be in later.'

'Give him my love. Tell him…' I didn't know what to say. 'Oh, just tell him I'll be there as soon as I can.'

I hung up and stared, longingly, at the wine bottle I hadn't opened. It was a temptation I resisted. 'Andy!' I shouted, as I ran up the stairs.

*

Both the kids went very quiet. I could recognize the torment within them. I thought briefly about my parents and the car crash that had killed them. I had been quite a lot older than these two, but you can never prepare for that kind of shock. They had already lost one parent; before I left the house I had to make absolutely certain they knew they weren't about to lose the other.

Andy and I exchanged a momentary glance that said so much about our own loss, before I started to stress that Derek was a bit cut and had a broken leg, but *that was all*!

'Can we come with you?' The inevitable question from Sarah.

'No, I don't think so. He just wanted me to bring some stuff in for tonight. He'll be home tomorrow.' I added the last part not knowing if it was true or not. I hadn't taken in everything the sister had said, but it would do for now. 'He's probably a bit of a mess, and he won't want you to see him like that. No doubt it looks ten times worse than it is. He sent his love and said he'll see you tomorrow.' I was compounding my lie, but it seemed the right thing to do. It had the desired effect.

'Okay,' Sarah said, quietly. 'Tell him I love him.'

'And me,' Tony added.

I swallowed hard and glanced at Andy, but before I asked the question he spoke.

'Good job I'm not going out, then. Go on, bugger off, he's probably waiting for his toothbrush.'

I raced around, grabbing some odds and ends, and ran down the stairs. Andy followed me. At the door he gave me a big hug. No words were necessary. As I hurried to the car I heard him shout, 'Hey, you two, get down here. Quick! I think there's an aardvark in the garden!'

Hilary's number was already ringing on my mobile before I had pulled out of the drive.

'Hello?'

'It's me. Derek's been involved in a car crash.'

There was a couple of seconds' silence. My best friend knew all the implications of that statement.

'Oh God, Ally, no! How bad?'

'They say he's a bit cut around the face, and he's got a broken leg.'

'Where are you now?'

'On my way to the hospital.'

'On your own?'

'Yes, Andy's with the kids. I think they're okay.'

There was a longer pause. 'And how are *you*?'

'All right, I think. It was, well…when I first heard…'

'I know, I know.' She waited a moment then said, 'Ally, take a deep breath…take another one. Now tell me exactly where you are. Which road are you on? Is there much traffic about? Are there any cyclists? Are those lights red or green?'

After a long pause I replied, 'I'm okay, and the lights were green anyway,' I told her.

I heard her breathe out.

'And there aren't any cyclists about, so you can shut up!'

I was aware of a chuckle.

'Do you want me to come to the hospital?'

'God, I hope not.' I concentrated for a moment to overtake a learner driver.

'I will if you want, you know I've nothing better to do!'

I smiled slightly. 'Your social life is a joke! Tell you what, I'll phone if the doctor's worth attacking.'

'You'd better! And make sure he's a little younger than Les. I think he was the last person you tried to set me up with!'

At that we both laughed. I wondered how I was so lucky to have a friend who knew me so well, and always knew exactly what I needed to hear.

'These sodding lights are red,' I told her.

'Well done, just keep concentrating on them.'

I took the deep breath. 'I really am okay, thank you.'

'So who's going to be the carer when he comes home?'

'Guess who isn't?' I retorted. 'At least I won't have two helpers with me at work.'

'It was that good, eh?'

'Worse! Sarah even started questioning me about my relationship with Mark.'

'That must have been an interesting conversation.'

'I think it went something like, Mind your own business!'

I heard Hilary chuckling as I pulled into the hospital car park and parked somewhere that probably wasn't even a space.

'*I'd* like a definitive answer on your relationship with Mark,' she said.

'We might need a whole weekend.'

'Okay, see you on Friday. I'll keep two days clear.'

I burst out laughing. Then a thought struck me. 'Shit! We were supposed to be going away on a boat,' I said. 'I guess that's out of the question with a broken leg.'

'You daft bat! Be grateful, you didn't want to go on the boat, anyway.'

I climbed from the car, still smiling, and walked towards the hospital entrance.

Chapter 10

'My name's Alison Sheldon. Someone phoned me from A&E. My boyfriend, Derek Lee, was brought in after a car accident.'

I recalled, a long time afterwards, quite how calm and matter of fact I had sounded, just stating the necessary facts – no hysteria. I should have realized that calmness was entirely inappropriate when I was directed, almost immediately, to the relatives' room and asked to wait.

An attractive-looking white-coated doctor entered. 'Alison?' he inquired.

I looked up at him and smiled, with a nod, and instantly thought I'd better rush out and phone Hilary – a thought that was to haunt me for a very long time.

'Alison. I'm Doctor Sharpe.' He paused for a moment. 'I'm afraid I have some bad news for you.'

Even then, I had no idea what he was about to say. Stupid thoughts like I hadn't brought enough clothes, or that actually both legs were broken, flashed through my mind.

The pause became elongated, and it was then that the first stab of panic hit me. Blindness was my first thought. They had said he was cut about the face, and I knew he wouldn't be able to cope with blindness. More to the selfish point, I knew *I* couldn't cope with blindness. Yet another dose of guilt I would have to learn to live with.

'Derek suffered severe shock from the accident,' the dishy doctor continued, 'and we think there may have already been a problem that he was probably unaware of.'

I stared at him. Suddenly the enormity of what he was trying to say began creeping into my flippant thoughts.

'The shock triggered a massive heart attack.'

The flippancy vanished with an icy feeling that seared through my entire body. I needed to ask him to repeat what he'd just said, but no sound came out of my mouth. Derek was forty-two. Forty-two-year-olds didn't have heart attacks. Fit, healthy, non-smoking forty-two-year-olds didn't have heart attacks.

I realized the doctor had sat down beside me. 'We did everything we could, but we weren't able to save him. Derek died about half an hour ago. I'm very sorry.'

'No!'

This wasn't happening. I wasn't going to believe this. This had to be some sort of horrible mistake. I wanted to say, Are you sure it's Derek? I wanted to tell him to go back and try to do something else: give him an electric shock, thump his chest, pump him full of whatever…just do *something*.

'I really am very sorry, Alison. Is there someone we can call for you?'

'No,' I said again, not quite certain what I was saying no to – the doctor's question, or the fact of Derek's death.

'Derek named you as his next of kin…'

'But I'm not!'

'He put you on the form.'

'He's got two children. And there's a brother somewhere, I think.'

Some time, in the preceding few minutes, a nurse had entered the room. I was suddenly aware that she had taken hold of my hand. I stared blankly at her, as if she didn't really exist. She had such a kind, sympathetic expression, and as our eyes met she gave my hand a gentle squeeze. I remembered her face, very often, in the days to follow, and I have wished, many times since, that I had said thank you. What I did say became another ghost that would haunt me.

'I don't know what to do with two kids!'

I became aware that the doctor was speaking again.

'...we need to carry out a post-mortem. I think we'll find that there may have been a heart abnormality, but we need your permission, as next of kin, to do that.'

'No! I can't do that!'

'Well, as a sudden death...'

'*Please*,' I interrupted. I stared at him, begging him to stop. I wanted to say, You've just told me Derek is dead, and now you want me to tell you it's all right to cut him into pieces! But all I heard myself say was, 'Can I see him?'

'Yes, of course you can.'

The kind face led me from the relatives' room to a stark, impersonal cubicle off a buzzing accident and emergency area. Raised voices, occasional shouts of pain and the general frenetic bustle of ridiculously busy people wafted unnoticed over me. It meant nothing.

He simply looked as if he was sleeping. His face wasn't that cut. I assumed they'd cleaned him up, but it was only a few scratches. I kept expecting him to open his eyes and smile at me. Eventually, I stretched out a slightly shaky hand and softly touched his cheek. Already, it wasn't as warm as it should have been.

Derek wasn't going to open his eyes and smile at me – ever again.

A voice from a long way off said gently, 'Stay as long you like.'

I found I had sat down. I heard the door close behind me, and I felt so horribly alone. I stared at his face as he lay there, eyes closed, at peace, and all the memories flooded back to me…

*

'You must be Alison. Hello, I'm Derek.' And I had started to cry.

'Is everything all right?'

I thought that was a pretty stupid question. Obviously everything wasn't all right, but I just mumbled, 'I'm sorry.' Then, to confuse him even more, I added, 'You're late!'

He didn't reply. He must have thought that if five minutes' tardiness had created this effect, it probably would have been better if he hadn't come at all.

I couldn't explain how I felt. He was a stranger. I nearly said to him that if he hadn't shown up it would have been even worse. Five minutes was enough for me to think he wasn't coming.

Just like before.

I had forced myself to come here, to sit on this very seat. This man was only five minutes late. Rob never showed up at all. Rob never showed up ever again.

Derek stood in front of me. I didn't look up, but I could sense his discomfort. I stared down at his white training shoes. They were clean; Rob's were always dirty. He cleared his throat. 'It might help to knock the hell out of a squash ball.'

I got to my feet, trying to keep the tears at bay. 'You're right, it might. I am sorry.'

'I don't normally have that effect on people,' he said, as he opened the door of the court.

I glanced across at him and endeavoured to find a smile. He had a kind face, through a full, neat beard. His hair was dark, but the beard was showing traces of grey. I couldn't guess his age. 'I don't normally react like that to people,' I answered, by way of another apology. At that moment I was certain that that would be the full extent of any explanation he ever received.

'Jenny on the desk said you hadn't played for a few months. I phoned to see if she could find me someone to have a game with. I lost my usual partner. He moved to North London.'

I couldn't reply to that. The thought that ran through my head was that I had lost my partner as well. He had moved too – right out of my life – taking my heart and soul with him.

'I know,' I managed eventually, 'she told me when she called.'

I beat him three games in a row. Actually it was more of an annihilation. Perhaps it was the first time that my grief over Rob had turned to anger. I took it out on a squash ball and a poor, unsuspecting stranger. All in all, he probably wondered why he did show up that evening. I think he was relieved when we heard a tap on the door.

We relinquished the court to the next booking and walked back towards the changing rooms.

'Would you like a drink?'

I felt a bit more in control by then. The manic physical activity had helped. A drink would mean talking, and talking might lead to explanations, and that wasn't going to happen. I wanted to play squash again regularly, and I needed to do it without all the associations of the past.

'I think it might be best if I said no, but maybe we can arrange another game and have a drink after that, if you'd like to?'

He smiled. It wrinkled up his brown eyes in a gentle way. 'That sounds good to me. Same time next week?'

At least tonight I didn't have to leave the squash courts bewildered, panic-stricken, not knowing what had happened and all too aware that I couldn't phone Rob's home to find out. Neither would I go home tonight and find that letter waiting for me. I knew, though, that I would go home and see the letter again, in my head. I also knew that the tears I'd shed earlier would be nothing compared with those that its memory would bring.

Maybe I should simply take up another sport. Maybe I would never be able to play squash again without the past assaulting me. But it hadn't really been because of the squash... A rare meeting at work had made me go straight to the court without going home first, as I usually did. I had changed, sat on that seat and waited. It wasn't the first time in our relationship that I had sat and waited – and waited – with my stomach turning over in fear. I had still been there when the next pair arrived for the court.

There had always been a reason, if he didn't turn up, and I knew he couldn't always let me know straightaway, but getting through the hours until he did had nearly destroyed me every time. That night, though, the reason had been waiting for me, in his neat handwriting, when I got home. He hadn't wanted me to sit on that seat, outside a squash court, and wait. He had wanted me to know in advance, and try to create a new life from that day, and deal with it in the way he undoubtedly knew I would – with a numbing, excessive dose of alcohol, and Hilary.

I wished I could hate him.

One week after my tearful attempt to return to the squash courts, I had forced myself to sit on that seat again, and my new life had begun.

'You must be Alison. Hello, I'm Derek.' He said it again and I suppose in my mind I thanked him for pretending that last week had never happened. Maybe we both needed to pretend that. I won the game, but it was close. I don't think I ever played, again, the way I had done the week before. I doubt Derek was too upset about that! We showered, changed and went for a drink in the bar. No mention was ever made of our previous meeting.

After a few weeks the drink progressed to a meal afterwards, and then that became the pattern. We chatted effortlessly. I felt I was beginning to know everything about his life, yet I was still holding back one aspect of mine. I was at ease with him, rather than feeling anything particularly intense. I really enjoyed our evenings, and having put a sealed lid on the box that held the most painful piece of my past, I could talk to him about anything. There was no doubt that Derek had rescued me.

The first tentative kiss good night on the cheek had moved on to a speculative one on the lips, which one day became a lingering kiss. That was the day he first asked me to go out with him the following Saturday. That Saturday was the day he appeared clean-shaven and looking a lot younger; the day I stayed the night for the first time; the day I cried in front of him again, then took the lid off the box and let out my past.

As a lover, he was very gentle and considerate. There was none of the frenetic passion of stolen moments that I'd longed for in previous years. He didn't have to keep checking his watch. We made love, and there were no questions about whether we had time to have a drink afterwards. I didn't have to meet him in odd, out-of-the-way places, or wait while he searched the faces of people in a bar to see if he knew them. I could phone Derek at home; I could even leave a message. We could walk down any road together; we could bump into friends of his and I could be introduced. I could even phone him at work and give my own name!

Yes, he had rescued me. He had given me the relationship that I'd never had, the relationship that I had longed for, but never had – with Rob. I may have taken the lid off the box, but the depth of feeling within it had never been fully released.

*

Suddenly I felt very cold, just like the man beside me, who had gone from my life equally as suddenly. I reached out and placed my hand over his. I found myself wondering, if time had allowed, would I ever have found that same intensity of feeling towards Derek? And I couldn't shake off the strange thought that, if I had, somehow, he might not be lying here now.

Chapter 11

'Hilary, *please* be there.'

It was the answerphone again. I'd tried it three times, probably in as many minutes. She'd said she wasn't doing anything! I tried her mobile again, but it was still switched off. Where the hell was she?

I had no recollection of walking out of the hospital.

I would have to leave a message. So far I'd resisted doing that. I didn't know what to say. I had just kept dialling her number and praying she would pick it up.

I dialled again. Two rings and her message greeted me once more.

'It's me, phone me please, whatever the time.'

As I disconnected my mobile rang. I dropped it in shock. It bounced to the floor of the car, where I was sitting, staring through the windscreen. I scrabbled under the seat for it, its inappropriately cheerful ring tone still playing. It was Andy.

'Hi, just checking to see how things are.'

I couldn't speak.

'Ally? You still there?'

'Yes,' I managed to say. 'Derek's dead.'

'*What?*'

'He had a heart attack.' I still couldn't believe what I was telling him. 'They think he must have had a heart problem. The shock was too much.'

It was my brother's turn to be speechless. After a long pause he said, 'Do you want me to tell the kids?' It was brave of him; I could hear the fear in his voice.

'No, I'll do it.'

'What shall I say…'

'I don't know!' I snapped at him. 'Tell them I'm waiting to see the doctor or something.' I took a deep breath. 'I'll be home soon.'

'Take care,' he said, quietly.

I found an old packet of cigarettes in the glove compartment and lit one, shakily. It tasted foul. They had probably been there for years.

I tried Hilary once more, unsuccessfully. How was I going to tell the kids? I'd said he was going to be all right. How were they going to cope with losing both parents? Where would they live? What the hell was I going to do with them? They couldn't live with me! I didn't want them living with me! But I might have to have them for the rest of the summer, before they went back to boarding school. But they didn't live at boarding school. They'd have no home. Did Derek even have enough money to pay for boarding school? What normally happened to orphans at their age? There had to be some organization that dealt with this sort of situation. I couldn't deal with it. I couldn't!

I pressed redial on my phone again, silently begging Hilary to respond. 'Jesus Christ, where are you?' I shouted out loud at the inevitable answerphone message. Why did she have to vanish tonight? I kept telling her to get a life, but why did she have to do it right now? Why, when I needed her? I could have phoned other people, but it was Hilary I needed to talk to. I had to. There was no way I could face those children before I'd spoken to her.

I lit another stale cigarette. This one tasted a little better. Maybe I could phone Mark? I shook my head at the thought. As close as we were, he wasn't the right person. I would have to phone him later, or in the morning anyway. And what the hell was I going to do about work? God, I didn't need this!

My mobile rang. With a jump, I peered at the name of the caller. A huge wave of relief flooded through me. 'Hilary, thank God!'

I don't know how I drove home.

I didn't remember a single set of traffic lights, or a T-junction or a right turn, or anything; I just remember suddenly finding myself pulling into the drive. My only memories were of being blasted, on more than one occasion, by irritated motorists behind me, because I was driving too slowly. But it wasn't slowly enough. I had arrived.

I sat in the car and stared at the house. The house that was precisely one third mine, because I had lost my parents in a car crash. Phil, Andy and I had coped – somehow – but we had other lives. You expect to lose your parents eventually; that's the nature of things. We had lost ours sooner than we should have done, but we were all adults. Inside were two young children who had already lost their mother, and now I had to go inside and tell them that I had lied to them. I had told them their father was okay. I had told them that he was coming home tomorrow. Inside were two kids who adored him, needed him, relied on him. He was their one piece of stability in a world that had gone mad for them. I looked to the skies, and said out loud, 'God, what have they done to deserve this?'

I lit another stale cigarette. I didn't know how to do this. This wasn't what I had planned for my life. I couldn't cope. I didn't want children. I didn't know how to deal with children. I wasn't like the nurse in the hospital, who could have held their hands and given them some sort of comfort. What if they wanted to go back and see him? They were bound to want to. Did I have to go back with them? Did I have to look at him again? Did I have to take their hands and go back into that bleak cubicle?

And what about me? Who was going to hold my hand for the rest of my life?

I restarted the engine. In that moment, I was going to turn round and drive out. I think, if I had done, no one would ever have found me. For many days after that, I regretted my hesitancy. I actually got into reverse gear, and then a car pulled up beside me. It was Hilary. Even then, I nearly drove away. We stared at each other and I think she knew what I was about to do. She made absolutely no move, just held the gaze between us. And then I flung open the door and almost fell out. She was out of her car in a second. She said nothing, just grabbed me and held me as tightly as she could.

'What do I say? What am I going to do with them? They haven't got any other family.'

Hilary pushed me away, still holding my shoulders. 'Ally, what about you?'

'I don't know.'

She let go of me and reached into my car, turned off the engine and removed the keys.

'I was going,' I told her.

'I know you were. But you'd never have forgiven yourself.'

'Maybe I would have done – eventually.'

She took my arm and steered me towards the house. At the front door she stopped and looked at me. 'I'll tell them, if you want.'

I shook my head, not thinking until days later that I should have thanked her for the offer.

'Just go and pour me a large drink!'

I put my key in the lock. I was afraid that both kids would rush out at the sound of the front door, but it was Andy's head that peered round from the lounge to greet me.

'How are you doing? We heard a car. The kids are in the garden. I told them it was Phil.' He registered Hilary and nodded to her. She walked past him and went to carry out my request. Andy inclined his head, waiting for an answer.

'Terrified,' I muttered.

'I'm afraid I didn't know what to say, so I said nothing.'

'That's okay, but would you come and hold Sarah's hand?'

'Of course I will.'

Hilary reappeared with a drink, which I took gratefully. I took a large mouthful, looked for a long moment at my best friend and then walked into the lounge and out into the garden. The other two followed. Before I had a chance to register the eager faces of two kids, who had suddenly realized who had arrived, Andy had gently taken hold of Sarah's hand and sat down beside her, and Hilary had sat down beside Tony.

It was a bright summer evening. There we were, on the patio, with drinks in our hands. And I was about to deliver the worst news these children would ever hear.

Sarah looked at me and instantly turned to her brother. 'Tony, we need some more crisps. Go and get them and then Ally can introduce us to her friend.'

The unsuspecting eleven-year-old nodded and ran indoors. His sister should not have had to have that much perception.

'He's dead, isn't he?' she said.

I simply nodded.

'I'll tell him,' Sarah said, and hastily got to her feet.

I took a breath to say – I'm not sure what – but she'd gone.

I don't recall how long it was before they reappeared. It felt like hours. In that time no one in the garden had said a word. I felt a complete coward. I hadn't had the courage to say what had happened. I had left it to another child to explain, and she hadn't even got any of the facts. I hadn't even registered what Derek's death had meant to me, but as I sat there, all I could think about was the kids. That thought made me realize that perhaps it didn't mean quite as much as it should have done. Then all I felt was a complete shit!

I had been fond of him, but he wasn't the love of my life, and he probably never would have been. We were comfortable and I enjoyed his company. Was I simply using him to forget Rob? Or was I simply using him? I had had so many doubts about Derek and the kids coming to stay. Were the doubts about having the kids, who I knew I didn't really want here, or were the doubts about Derek and our relationship?

I thought of my life as it was – or rather as it had been a couple of hours ago – and asked myself if I was happy. The only honest answer was no. The job was okay, sometimes, and it paid me enough. The people I worked with were brilliant, most of the time. My social life was fun. I loved the band. I had some very special friends. I lived in the house I wanted to live in. I was independent. I did my own thing. I had two great brothers I got on with, but there was an undeniable void in my life.

People sometimes say that there is only one person for each of us in this world, and I had lost mine long before tonight. Derek had been a substitute. Maybe even the kids had been part of that substitution too.

I had tried so hard to forget Rob that I had used anything, and anyone, to achieve that end. Maybe, until that moment, I had never been completely honest with myself about my own feelings. Maybe that moment when Sarah had vanished to tell her brother the devastating news, that I should have had the courage to relate myself, was the first time I had really taken stock of my life. Derek had been second best. His kids represented something I swore I never wanted, but, in truth, I probably would have done, had their father been someone else.

I'm not sure who felt worse when Sarah and Tony reappeared, but I know that my feelings of guilt outweighed everyone else's.

Tony stopped in front of me. I saw the pain and bewilderment on his young face and I had never hated myself so much.

'You said he would be home tomorrow!'

'I honestly believed he would be. That's what the hospital told me.'

'But you promised!'

'I made a promise I shouldn't have, because someone made that promise to me.' I despised myself for my reply. 'Tony, I've lost someone special too.'

'It's not the same for you!'

Out of the mouths of babes…

I didn't know what to do, or say, so I simply extended my arms. He hurled himself towards me and buried himself in my enveloping hug. I felt his sobs through my chest. Out of the corner of my eye I was aware that Andy had put an arm around Sarah, who was crying with much more self-control.

I couldn't even bear to look towards Hilary. At that moment, I wanted to push Tony away and walk out. Derek may not have been Rob, but this was still a hell of a shock.

He may have been second best, but maybe one day he wouldn't have been. We had never had the time to find out. I hadn't given Derek a real chance because I hadn't stopped feeling sorry for myself about Rob, and now that chance was gone. Maybe if I had been less involved with myself, and a little more involved with him, this wouldn't have happened. As I entertained that thought, I realized it was probably rubbish. I was an expert at beating myself up emotionally, and I was doing it again. And yet, maybe there might have been something in it. Had Rob said, Let's go and book a boating holiday, I would have thought, Stuff work, and gone with him. Would that have made any difference?

Tony suddenly registered as an unwanted heavy weight on me. I eased him away. Reluctantly, he got the message, but he grabbed his chair and pulled it as close as he could to mine.

'What actually happened?' Andy said at last, breaking a very long silence.

'He had a heart attack. They think he already had a problem, but no one knew about it.' There was nothing else I could say.

I got up and walked indoors for another drink. Hilary followed me. I topped up my glass with hands that were anything but steady, then turned round and looked at her. I felt about five years younger than Tony. I needed someone to tell me none of this was true; to change what had happened; to make it all better; to take the nightmare away.

'I can't do this,' I said, and I wished the tears would start; not for the kids, not for Derek, but for me.

Chapter 12

For those first few seconds, as I woke up, the world was fine. It was just another ordinary day. And then I remembered. The world was anything but fine. It was far from being just another ordinary day. It was the day after my world had been turned upside down. I looked towards the window. It was dark outside. It matched how I felt: cold, empty and black. I could still hardly believe what had happened; all the events of yesterday evening still felt unreal. This was the third time in a little over five years that I had woken up with the same feelings of loss and unreality, and the child in me wanted to stamp her foot and whine that it simply wasn't fair! One person can only take so much, and the self-pity started to make me wonder what the hell would go wrong next. But this disaster was far from resolved. It wasn't just my world that had fallen apart; there were two kids to think about, and that made it a thousand times worse. I turned my head to see the clock and discovered it was 1.43. Why couldn't I have slept through the night, at least?

I felt numb. Maybe if I could cry it would help, but there were no tears. Perhaps I could get angry, and scream and throw things, but there was no anger either. I didn't feel anything, just an urge to be anywhere but right where I was at that moment, and a wish that some miracle would whisk the kids away, so I didn't have to face them again – probably, ever again.

I tried turning over, closing my eyes and hoping that sleep would return, but it was a vain hope. After what seemed like hours, I got up. I dragged on a dressing gown, thought, Bugger it, to whoever I disturbed and, turning on the landing light, went downstairs. I made myself a coffee and poured a ridiculously large brandy, then sat, hugging the glass, staring into the blackness of the garden.

I just felt utterly bewildered. I needed to ask so many questions, but would I ever get any of the answers? 'Dear God, what *is* happening to me? What is this all about? Do I somehow deserve this? Have I screwed up so much that this is some sort of punishment? How many more people I care about are going to be taken from me? How many more losses am I going to have to live through? I wanted someone to run to who would make it all better. I wanted my mum.

I stared at the drink in my hands. It would never provide the solution, but it was the thing I always ran to now, wasn't it? It was a pathetically poor substitute. I took another swig of that substitute and tried asking myself rational questions. What do people normally do in these circumstances? But this wasn't normal. There was no formula for how to deal with this kind of situation; no tried and tested method that would work for everyone. I knew people who had lost their partners – admittedly, none had been close friends, so I guess I didn't see the reality of what went on behind closed doors – but they seemed to cope, eventually. I hadn't been able to learn from my parents how either of them survived without the other, because they had gone together. Lucky for them, I thought, sourly. I didn't know anyone of my own age who had been in this situation, and no one who had had any children to deal with. I had suddenly lost my boyfriend of a little over a year. That fact alone was hard enough to deal with, but I had his children to think of and get through this. Not *my* children, or *ours*, but *his*! I barely even knew them. I'd never seen them upset or had to deal with a grazed knee, or an argument with a best friend, or the loss of a pet hamster. I didn't know anything about dealing with children. I'd never had to cope with their tears and anxieties, even on a minor level, let alone something as devastating as this. I'd experienced things that felt like the end of the world when I was their age, but I'd had a mum or a dad to run to. Now they didn't have either, and neither did I.

I needed to cry; I needed to get angry; but, as yet, neither the tears nor the anger would come. There was just a creeping sense of guilt that I couldn't shake. I wasn't tired enough to sleep, but I was too tired to figure out if the guilt was simply that I might have made a difference, had I been in the car with Derek, or the knowledge that maybe I just didn't care enough about him.

Suppose he had been the love of my life? Suppose I had been with him? It might be that I would be in hospital now, or even dead. Had I cared about him with the intensity that I did about Rob, and worried when he was driving, or flying, or going anywhere for that matter – would that have made any difference? I shook my head and stared out into the garden.

No, of course it wouldn't, I told myself, although the doubt and the guilt remained.

I couldn't face going down that route, so I got up and turned the garden lights on so I could see beyond the oppressive blackness. Something four-legged ran away. 'It's probably a bloody aardvark,' I muttered to myself.

I noticed my glass was empty, so I rectified that and sat down again, and thought about two kids. I might have lost someone – suddenly, violently and unexpectedly – but whatever I felt about Derek, I hadn't lost everything that mattered to me in the world. They had.

The guilt kicked me in the guts with a vengeance. Had he meant that much, I would have thought I'd just lost everything, and it would have taken Hilary to keep telling me that I hadn't to keep me going. I stood up, suddenly angry with myself. He hadn't just been a casual friend I occasionally had sex with. I *did* love him. It was nearly three in the morning, and here I was, sitting, drinking alone, beating myself up about the depth of my affection for my boyfriend who had died just a few hours ago.

That's when I started to cry. I think the shock and the brandy both hit me at the same time, and I crumpled into a heap on the sofa.

I've no idea how long I was there, but a voice suddenly broke through the sobs.

'I saw the garden lights. Can I help?' It was Andy.

'Fuck off,' I replied.

'Are you sure?'

'Yes! No… I don't know… Sorry.'

'Want another drink?'

I looked down, the glass was empty again. I nodded.

'And coffee?'

'Yes, please.'

I was calmer by the time he reappeared. We spent our lives winding each other up, but not this time. He put the mugs and glasses on the table and I leapt to my feet, to be wrapped in a huge hug from one of the few people I was sure of. When we finally let go of each other, he ruffled my hair.

'Piss off,' I said, with little conviction, but it made him smile.

'Dear God,' he muttered, 'save us from builders' language.'

I looked up at him and smiled, through blurred eyes. 'Thanks…Richard!'

I think that maybe that was one of the most meaningful moments in my relationship with my younger – often irritating – brother. We just sat in the room together. We didn't have to say anything. He was there for me and I knew it. He wanted to be there for me, and I knew that as well. Phil and I had a sort of understanding that was special. Maybe because he was my big brother, and someone I had always run to for guidance, or maybe simply because he was older, and had probably already made every mistake that I was about to make. Andy was younger than me, and the relationship was different. He still had Phil to follow, but there was an annoying female that came above him in the pecking order. I couldn't give him advice, and I wouldn't turn to him for advice either. Phil had a little sister to annoy, if he felt like it, but Andy had no one to torment who was younger than him. Somehow, over the years, we had found ways of tormenting each other. It was never really malevolent, but it served both our purposes in terms of sibling rivalry.

At that moment, I wanted to apologize for every rude thing I had ever said to him. At that moment, I think he knew that and maybe he felt the same way. Nothing was said, but after an age of silence, we both glanced at each other and got up simultaneously for another hug.

We would still torment each other, but from that day, we both knew it had a slightly different meaning. I think we both grew up a bit that morning. My boyfriend had died, but a part of my family life had changed because of it. My eyes filled up again as I realized that Derek would never know of that special moment that he had given to Andy and me.

'What needs to be done today?' Andy asked.

'God, I don't know.' My whole insides turned over at the thought of everything I would have to do. The running away option reared its head again.

'Did Derek have any family?'

'Not really. His parents are dead. There's a brother somewhere, in Australia I think, but beyond that I haven't a clue.'

'What about the wife?'

I took a deep breath and let it out, slowly. 'Well, she's been dead for some time, as you know. Her parents are still alive, but I don't think the kids have seen them much since their mother died.'

I couldn't say anything else, for a moment. A feeling of total disbelief about what they had suffered swirled through my head.

'Tony's sort of okay about them, but Sarah seems to blame them for all sorts of things, probably including their mother's death.'

'How come?'

'Oh, I'm guessing really, only she was pretty vindictive about them the other day. Derek says...' I stopped, hearing what I'd said. I swallowed and made myself go on. 'Derek used to say that they probably made his wife worse. They were old school, particularly the father. They couldn't, or wouldn't, accept that she might be depressed. That would have been too much of a slur. It was too close to mental illness. Their attitude was, You made your own bed, you lie in it. She was supposed to find the strength to deal with her own problems. They were certainly no help to her. And they never accepted that she committed suicide.'

'Is that definite?'

'Oh, yes. The coroner's verdict didn't leave room for any doubt. The parents made a lot of noise about suing the garage that serviced her car, as the brakes must have failed, but no one else was in any doubt that she drove off the cliff herself. The kids obviously heard all the fuss the grandparents were making, and Derek just let them hear it. It gave them a chance to call it an accident if they wanted to, but they don't think it was an accident either.'

'They seem to have dealt with it pretty well.'

'I know, but this…' The tears started to well up again.

Andy stared at the floor for a moment. 'Not easy,' he muttered. 'Another drink?'

I nodded. 'I'll make the coffee.'

*

We were still sitting there well after the sun came up. Phil joined us. He said nothing in particular, just arrived in the room and changed the order from coffee and brandy to tea and cooked breakfast. Phil never cooked breakfast. He'd always eat it, when it was on offer, but he never cooked it. This whole event seemed to have brought what remained of my family closer together.

The doorbell rang just after 7.30. It was Hilary. Apart from my earlier tears, I had been okay, talking to Andy for hours. I let her in, called to Phil to add one more plate of bacon and eggs and then completely lost it. Brothers were one thing, but your best friend, who knows everything about your life, was something else.

I have no idea what I said to her. I cried. I rambled on incoherently and cried some more, and in all that time she never let go of me. The friend who had shared my life since we were eleven finally released her grip on me as my big brother appeared with a tray of hot food, which was the last thing that I wanted.

I think I ate bits of it, or maybe I just played with it. I believe some sort of conversation was going on while I was trying. I just remember being immensely relieved that the kids hadn't come downstairs. It never occurred to me that that was strange. I chased a piece of bacon round my plate and became aware that Hilary was speaking.

'Sorry, what did you say?'

Hilary waited a moment before repeating her comment. 'What did Mark say?'

My eyes widened as I stared at her. 'Oh my God,' I said, at last.

'You haven't told him?'

I continued to stare.

Hilary stood up. 'I'll phone him if you want.'

'No, I think I'd better do it.' I looked at the clock. Mark was probably already preparing mugs of tea, in anticipation of my arrival.

It wasn't the easiest phone call I'd ever made, but it was probably the least stressful one I would make that day. I simply told him the facts, managed to hold myself together and left him to sort out the work. He said he'd call later, and I hung up. A brief panic about the job flashed through me, but I made myself ignore it. When I went back to the kitchen I realized that the kids had still not appeared.

Hilary seemed to sense my thoughts. 'Have you spoken to them this morning?'

'No, they're normally up long before this.'

What, I asked myself, would two children, whose mother had committed suicide, think about doing, when everything they cared about had been suddenly taken away?

Hilary followed me up the stairs. I hadn't voiced my fears, but I guess I'd transmitted them, nevertheless. My knock on Sarah's door received no answer and I opened it with a horrible sinking feeling. It was empty. Hilary and I exchanged glances, and we moved along to Tony's room. I didn't bother with knocking this time, but as we entered the room, the sinking feeling turned to panic. All I could see was blood.

Sarah leapt to her feet. 'I'm so sorry,' she gabbled, 'I didn't know what to do. I'll clear it up, honest, and I'll wash the sheets.'

I think my mouth must have dropped open, but before I could even inquire what had been going on, Tony, complete with blood-stained tissue across his face, ran across the room and grabbed hold of me.

'He kept crying, and blowing his nose, and then it started bleeding, and I couldn't stop it, and there's such a mess...'

'Sarah, don't worry. There's no damage done. Really it's all right.'

'But it's not!' she said. 'It'll never be all right again!' And with that, she collapsed on the bed, amid the remains of Tony's nosebleed, and started to cry.

Chapter 13

I couldn't believe that you had to make an appointment to see the registrar. It was hard enough to do, without making it seem like some sort of business deal. I wanted to shout at the faceless woman on the phone, Hey, my boyfriend's just dropped dead, I'm sorry if this might be inconvenient for *you*!

Next, I came close to assaulting the spiky-haired young thug who looked like he was barely out of primary school and was more interested in talking to his girlfriend on the phone than giving me my boyfriend's death certificate. And why do personal effects always have to come in a black plastic sack? I made a mental note to write a vitriolic letter to the hospital about the staff who dealt with bereaved families, as I slammed out of the fire escape door. It had to be a back door, didn't it? Hardly the right image for a hospital, to have weeping people walking out of the front door, clutching a pamphlet on how to record a death and a dustbin liner!

The fact that the registrar had had an appointment that morning did not improve my view of the system. I couldn't even find the place, to begin with. A ridiculously small noticeboard, hidden by some overgrown clump of weeds, seemed to point into a housing estate, and then there was nowhere convenient to park. When I finally met the woman, she was dressed for a cocktail party, with far too much make-up, and her perfectly manicured nails were so long that she had trouble typing. She handed me a booklet about things that needed to be done, and – I think – was about to launch into a well-rehearsed speech about dealing with bereavement, and the help available.

'I know,' I all but snapped at her, 'I've done all this quite recently with my parents.'

She said something that I don't remember, which was probably sympathetic and appropriate, but I was too busy thinking that I actually couldn't remember all the things that needed to be done. I escaped as fast as I could, wishing that, at times, I could be a nicer person.

If I had been a nicer person, would Derek still be alive?

It was a relief to see Hilary's car still there when I got home. I had to drive to Derek's house and, presumably, this time, I would have to take the kids with me. I wondered if she'd agree to come, but I didn't even have to ask. When I gathered up the kids, she just collected her things and climbed into the car with us.

The motorway was almost at a standstill. I didn't need that on top of everything else. I looked at the next junction marker and tried to remember if I'd ever found an alternative route to Derek's on that road. Just as I decided that I had once tried and got hopelessly lost, the road cleared and the traffic ahead just moved off. I muttered and swore quietly through the entire journey, taking out some of my anger and frustration on other drivers. I thumped the wheel once, in temper, as we were faced with temporary traffic lights at a tiny back-road junction. I hit it so hard, I sounded the horn, and the woman in front looked round very indignantly. In the whole hour and three-quarters that the journey took, I never once thought about how the kids were feeling. I just knew that I didn't want to go where we were going. No one said a word the entire time, apart from my bad-tempered outbursts, until we pulled into the drive, and then Tony spoke.

'Can I stay in the car?' he asked hesitantly.

'If you'd prefer that, then yes,' Hilary answered.

I swung round, about to say something like, Hey, I don't want to be here either, you little coward, get in there with me! But I didn't. I suddenly realized it was me who was the coward. I didn't want to go in to a flood of sad memories, some of which were already reminding me of sorting through papers after my parents died, and I just didn't want to do it again.

I opened Derek's front door. A voice should have greeted me. A voice should have called out, You're late! He always said that, when I arrived, because I was never late. No voice sounded, but it did in my head. I walked through to the lounge. He should have been there, holding two glasses, because he'd seen me arrive. Sadly, two glasses stood on the coffee table, waiting to be put away. I walked into the kitchen. There should have been wonderful cooking smells wafting out. He was a great cook. On a sudden impulse, I opened the oven. A cold, clean roasting tray stared back at me. I swung round to march up to the bathroom, looking for the candle he'd lit, in case I wanted to soak in luxury while he finished preparing the meal and brought me a drink refill. Sarah was staring at me.

'You *did* care, didn't you?'

I couldn't reply. I just nodded, and fought back the tears. Finally I found my voice. 'Left it a bit late to realize, didn't I?'

'I'm sure Dad realized.'

I looked at her. Sometimes I hated this child. I should have been trying to console her, not the other way round. 'Sarah, there's some milk in the car, would you get it, and make us all some tea, please?'

She went without a word.

I thought that the bathroom was a really stupid place to visit, but I had to go anyway. And then I went into his bedroom. I knew I was being a masochist, but I had to complete my tour. It was the final straw. At that moment, I couldn't remember when the next time I had been due to visit might have been, but, there, on what had become my pillow, was a small, wrapped chocolate mint and a little red plastic rose.

When Hilary found me I was sitting on the bed, sobbing quietly.

She sat, without speaking, for some time, with her arm round my shoulders. Eventually she asked, 'Where do you want to start?'

I blew my nose. 'Papers, I suppose. Downstairs in the desk.'

I found the local directory and started to search for funeral directors. Suddenly, a thought struck me. Where should this funeral be? This was Derek's home, but he died near me. He was lying in a hospital near me. Did I have to sort out some reception for people I didn't know, in a house I didn't really know, or did I have to have my house full of grieving strangers – *and* kids!

I shut the book and stared at Hilary.

'Do you want me to do it?'

'It's not the doing it, it's *where* to do it.'

'Oh!' Then she caught on to my thought pattern. 'I should think it needs to be local to here.'

'He didn't die here,' I replied, sulkily. 'I can't deal with sorting out everyone back at this house.'

'You won't have to. Lots of people go to a pub afterwards or something like that.'

'I don't know any of the pubs round here.'

'Then pick one you do know.'

'So why have the funeral near here?'

'You don't have to, but there must be friends and neighbours, and wasn't his firm nearby?'

'I hardly know any of his friends, and I haven't a clue if he even spoke to his next-door neighbours.'

'Well, you do what you like. He lived here, it just seems logical to me.'

I hung my head. 'Sorry.'

She gave me a compassionate smile. 'No, I'm sorry. I can't even begin to imagine how hard this is.'

'I really can't face organizing everyone back here, and I don't want them at home either. We did all that for Mum and Dad. I can't do it again.'

'Well, let's just get the undertakers sorted out and worry about afterwards later.'

It was a tempting suggestion, but then I realized it was impossible. 'We can't. I'm going to have to start phoning people and everyone will want to know about the funeral. I'd have to phone them all again.'

I knew I was being awkward, and I could see she was getting frustrated, but I felt as if I couldn't make any decisions right now. That ability had vanished.

'Okay,' she said, attempting to remain patient, 'let's think about a pub.' She realized she wasn't going to get an answer, so she reached out for the local directory. Then she stopped. 'Phil's rugby club. They hire out the hall, don't they? And they've got a bar. And...' she went on, warming to her own suggestion, 'it's probably as near here as it is to you.'

I stared at her. 'That *is* a thought.'

'So, phone him.'

I looked at my watch. 'He's probably teaching.'

I think she was close to hitting me. 'So get them to drag him off the sports field. Tell them it's an emergency. It is, anyway!'

*

What would I do without Hilary?

By mid-afternoon I had rediscovered some organizational abilities and had sorted out an undertaker. I found the whole idea of getting quotes for burying a loved one rather distasteful. I was also aware of Sarah watching me when I told various people I was looking for a price for a 'modest' funeral. It was the term Phil had used for our parents, and at the time I'd thought it was rather a useful phrase, under the circumstances. I don't think she approved.

I had also made the difficult call to Derek's company, and notified his bank, but I still hadn't found any trace of an address or phone number for his brother. I had also shied away from phoning his friends, and definitely put off phoning his wife's parents. Instead I'd started looking through papers, and quickly felt I was being swamped by them. There were insurance companies and building societies, clubs he belonged to and God knows what else. Hopefully, when the bank stopped all the standing orders, that would let most of them know.

I turned round to speak to Hilary, who had been there moments before, but she'd disappeared. When I went to find her, I discovered that she, both kids and my car had gone! I knew she'd probably gone to find something to eat, as lunch was hours overdue, but I felt a momentary pang of fear, followed by the worst feeling of isolation I can ever remember.

I started opening Derek's recent mail. It had to be done, but it didn't stop me feeling guilty about reading his letters. The first was a credit card bill. Having no idea how that sort of thing got sorted out, I pushed it to one side, then suddenly a wave of panic hit me. He'd booked the boat! Where was I going to find the stuff about the boat? Would they charge, anyway? I couldn't even remember when we were supposed to be going, which proved how interested I'd been in the whole idea. Hopefully, Tony would remember.

It was then I realized that I hadn't found his will. I had absolutely no idea who the executor was, but maybe he, or she, should be doing some of this. Perhaps I shouldn't be doing it at all. He had mates; I could have left it to them. But his mates didn't have his kids, I did, and I had no idea what I was going to do with them.

I knew their grandparents weren't the nicest people on earth, but they were still their grandparents. Surely the kids were *their* problem, not mine. Well, they would simply *have* to be their problem. I couldn't have two kids to look after. Even if they were at boarding school, there were still holidays and half-terms, and it certainly wasn't my job to feed them or clothe them, or run to the school when they got in a scrape.

I got to my feet, wishing Hilary hadn't taken the car, in case there was anything left in that old, stale packet of cigarettes. No, the kids weren't my responsibility. If they threw a complete tantrum about their grandparents, then social services, or somebody, would have to sort it out. Surely that's what they were there for? That decided, I felt a little better, and carried on opening the letters. I wished I hadn't.

In many ways, it was a silly thing to reduce me to streams of tears. It wasn't as if I didn't know that he was trying to get tickets for this concert; it was simply that it was only really me that wanted to go. He had agreed to give it a try to find out what all the fuss was about. Deep down I think he probably hated country music, but it was what my band played and I went on about it constantly. This was an evening with various people, almost all American, that included artists and bands I'd wanted to see for years. Now, in my hand, were two of the most expensive concert tickets I'd ever held! I knew that I should really send them back and have Derek's card refunded, but I also knew I wouldn't. The conflict of emotions, on a scale of one to ten, was around fifteen when Hilary and the kids arrived back. As she opened the door, my feelings of guilt shot off the scale, as I realized I had actually been thinking about who to take with me! I must have looked like a frightened rabbit.

'What's happened?'

I shook my head. 'It's hard opening letters. I just found two tickets for Derek and me that he'd sent for.' It was a long time before I could admit, even to Hilary, what I'd been thinking.

Tony came in this time and walked over to me, and I gave him a hug. What else could I do? Hilary threw me a packet of cigarettes, then said, 'But I'll have one back, and if you remind me of that, at any time, you're finished!' We had both given up smoking on the same day, about two and a half years before.

I smiled in gratitude, surreptitiously stuffed the concert tickets into my handbag, and continued going through the papers from Derek's desk. By the time Sarah and Hilary had made sandwiches and more tea for a late lunch, I had found Derek's will.

Tony had decided he wanted to completely bury himself in my side, which made both reading the papers, and eating, almost impossible. About one nanosecond from me telling him to fuck off, Hilary called him over to give her a hand with clearing up the kitchen. Fortunately, blissfully, and very reluctantly on his part, he complied.

The executors, to my immense relief, were the solicitors who had set up the will. Now I could dump all these papers on them and let them sort it out. But I read it anyway, just in case.

Everything was left, equally divided, to Sarah and Tony. I felt a huge load lift from my shoulders. I had been afraid that he might have had a rush of blood to the head and included me, and I knew I would never have coped with the guilt that would have created. I read on, without really reading, the terms of the trust that had been set up for the kids, had Derek died when they were still minors, and wondered, sadly, if he *did* know that he had a heart problem. It would be typical of him that he knew and never told anyone. I asked myself how I would have felt if I'd been aware that I was going out with someone who was living on borrowed time. I didn't like my answer, and, on this occasion, the guilt brought a whole lot of tears in its wake.

Hilary appeared, uncannily on cue, and two more cigarettes went from the packet, but this time it made us giggle; and then the giggles became uncontrollable. I was very grateful that the kids were not in evidence. No one can ever explain the release of emotion and the route it takes.

Two young children were never going to understand why we were now crying with laughter on the day we had organized their father's funeral. I still recall Phil's then-wife, looking in complete disbelief at her husband and his two siblings playing a ridiculous game of charades the evening their parents died.

By late afternoon I had found a couple of old address books and loads of other bits of paper with names on – people who may or may not have been friends. Derek seemed to have more work numbers in his address book than home ones, so I had no way of knowing if these were clients or mates. I doubted that any of them would want to hear the news while sitting at their desks, if they were friends; but I still had not found his brother. To Tony and Sarah, Uncle James was little more than a name. They thought he was in Australia, as I did, but they weren't sure. I had started going through another pile of papers, in case I came across anything that might give me a clue, but, suddenly, I decided I'd had enough. We had to come back here the next day anyway, to make the arrangements with the funeral directors, and I certainly wasn't going to spend the night here. I was not going to spend a lonely night with a chocolate mint and a plastic rose and a tangle of emotions that I didn't know what to do with.

I got up from the desk. 'I can't do any more today Let's go home.'

Sarah looked at me. 'This *is* home,' she said.

I heard Hilary's intake of breath. I stared at Sarah, and thought of a thousand things to say – most of them extremely offensive. She held my gaze defiantly, almost daring me to reply. I felt I was being tested. I'd felt it before from her, when she questioned me about my relationships with Mark and her father. I didn't react well to confrontation; I always flared up in my own defence. Something about her, at times, made me flare up instantaneously. Obviously she was deeply upset, and presumably insecure, but she certainly knew how to get to me.

Finally I broke my gaze with her and turned to her brother. 'Come on, Tony, let's go.' I'm not certain, but I thought I heard him say, quietly, 'Where's home, now?' I ignored it, waved a hand, which he readily took, and we walked out, closing the door with a sort of slow finality that summed up the day.

The journey back was about ten times worse than the one down, and by the time we arrived my blood pressure would probably have registered a need for emergency treatment. Both Phil and Andy were there, which was a huge relief for me. They didn't say much, but that didn't matter. Phil made us all coffee, although I actually wanted a huge glass of wine instead.

Just as I decided that I was going to have one anyway, Hilary got to her feet and announced, 'I think I'd better go. I'll call you in the morning, and if you want some help tomorrow, I'm free in the evening.'

At that moment, something snapped. I couldn't face watching her leave. I ignored every consequence I was leaving behind. 'I'm coming with you,' I said. I grabbed my bag and followed her to the door. She made no comment. She didn't even look surprised. She just walked out to her car, with me in her wake. I didn't turn to see if either brother had a stunned expression on his face. I didn't turn to see if either of the kids had dissolved in tears. Hilary didn't look back. I didn't look back. By the time I was in her car it was already moving. We drove out like a Grand Prix start and neither of us said a word until we were inside her flat and halfway through a very, very stiff drink.

Chapter 14

If it had been irresponsible abandoning two grieving children, it was probably equally as bad to have jumped into Hilary's car as a means of escape. Now it was seven thirty in the morning and she had to drive me home before going to work. I offered to get a taxi, but she wouldn't hear of it. She pulled up at the gate, gave my arm a squeeze and said, 'Talk to you later.'

I nodded my appreciation and got out, then waited until she was out of sight before walking up the drive. We had a very long front garden, and I walked very slowly.

No, I shouldn't have run away last night, but at least I hadn't completely run away. The evening had been what I needed. We had talked very little about anything. Hilary had put on an old, sloppy film, and we'd let it waft over us, while consuming a lot of drinks. Now I had to face the kids, and maybe an irate brother or two, and get on with all the other things that needed doing.

I found Andy in the kitchen, which was a surprise at that time of day. He was dressed in suit, shirt and tie, so presumably he was meeting someone who needed to perceive him as mature.

'I trust you had a very pleasant evening.' The annoyance was undisguised.

Under any other circumstances I would have given some offensive reply, whether I was at fault or not. 'Sorry, I just needed to get away.'

'Well, thanks a million,' he responded, making the most of his advantage. 'Tell that to those two upstairs.'

'How were they?'

'How do you think they were?'

I'd done the apology bit, he wasn't getting any more. 'I don't know, Andy, that's why I'm asking you!'

He didn't answer that. 'And what would have happened if Phil or I had had to go out?'

'You'd have gone.'

Any further discussion was prevented from deteriorating into a full-scale argument by 'those two upstairs' appearing at the door. Tony was holding his sister's hand, which I found choked me a little. Andy gave me a glare and with a polite, 'Excuse me,' squeezed past the kids and vanished.

It was a daft question, but I asked it anyway. 'Are you all right?'

They both nodded, looking anything but all right. I decided against apologizing to them for my disappearing act. I might need to do it again.

'Would you like some tea?'

Two more nods.

'Sit down, then.' They were probably hungry. I had eaten at Hilary's, but I got out cereal and things and put them on the table. 'Is that okay?'

I got the same response. This was a very one-sided conversation.

I joined them at the table with my tea. 'I will have to go and sort out the funeral later today.'

'Are we going home again?' Sarah asked.

I was aware of her use of the word 'home', but just as I registered that thought, she spoke again.

'I mean, are we going to Dad's house?'

My awareness turned to unease. Was this another test? Was she climbing down after my reaction, yesterday, to her making a point of calling Derek's place her home, or was she now assuming that my place was home? If she was cleverly looking for some sort of clarification, she wasn't going to get it. I did my best to ignore that notion.

'No, not today.'

I knew I would have to go back, often, probably, but I couldn't face it again today.

I also knew I would have to start making endless phone calls, once I had a funeral date, time and venue, and maybe I would have to knock on a few doors too.

'I've got to go and talk to the undertakers and I must try to see the solicitors today, as well. I will need to call a lot of people to tell them about your Dad, but you'll have to tell me if there are any neighbours or friends in the road who ought to know.'

Sarah glanced at her brother, questioningly, but he just shrugged.

'There used to be an old lady next door, but I don't know if she's still there. Dad used to feed her cat sometimes.'

'Which side?'

'Number eleven. The couple the other side used to chat to Dad over the fence, but otherwise I'm not sure.'

'Don't you have mates round there?'

'We only moved there after Mum died.'

That was the first time I'd realized that. By then they were both at boarding school and their only mates were there. They weren't playing in neighbours' gardens or on the street. They had had that part of growing up taken away from them as well.

'There's Sammy,' Tony suddenly said.

'Is he a friend?'

Sarah smiled slightly. 'Not really, he's the old man that has the paper shop. Everyone calls him Sammy. He might know who Dad knew.'

She suddenly looked tearful. This was so hard for them. They were rarely at 'home'. They didn't know who Derek saw during the week, or who he chatted to, or whether he went for drinks with the neighbours. Here I was, trying to find out about Derek's life from them, and they knew as little as I did.

I got up to fetch the papers that I had brought back and they instantly stood up to follow me. After last night, I suppose it wasn't surprising.

'Stay there, I won't be a second. Make some more tea.'

I returned in less than a minute, but Tony was standing watching from the doorway, and he didn't sit down again until I did.

'I could do with knowing who some of these people are.' I started reading out names, but it was obvious they were going to be of no help. I think the only ones they recognized were the few that I knew.

I suddenly envisaged a crazy scenario.

'Hello, my name's Alison, are you a friend of Derek Lee?'

'Yes, I am, how is he?'

'Well, he's dead!'

No, I wasn't going to start that today!

On reflection, I decided that perhaps I did need to make just a small start. There were two of his friends I had met more than once. They didn't work with him, but the news might filter through, and it would be unkind to let them find out that way. I had work numbers; they would just have to put up with hearing the news sitting at their desks at nine o'clock in the morning. 'I must make some calls,' I said. I fetched the phone from the hall. Tony followed me out and followed me back. I really didn't think the kids were going to like this, but I couldn't exactly tell them to go away.

One ring and a curt voice answered, 'Jack O'Neil.'

'Jack, I don't know if you remember me, it's Alison, Derek's girlfriend. I'm afraid I have some bad news for you.'

Sarah rushed out of the room and Tony burst into tears.

I couldn't help either of them; I had a mate of Derek's hanging on for the next sentence. I must have paused longer than I thought, stunned by the kids' instant reaction, because a voice said in my ear, 'Hello? Alison?'

I waved an arm at Tony and he rushed to be held by it.

'I'm sorry, I've got Derek's kids here.' That probably made no sense to him. 'I'm afraid Derek died on Wednesday.'

I think I finished the call. Tony was a wreck and I had no idea where Sarah was. I needed to find her, but there was no way Tony was letting go of me, so it was both of us who discovered her in the garden. She looked a little tearful, but calmer.

'Perhaps Tony should stay here with me, if you have more calls to make,' she said.

I nodded. I couldn't speak. I was more wrung out than they were. Sooner or later she was going to fall apart and she needed to. The coward in me wasn't sure I wanted to be there when she did.

I made my calls, including one to the solicitors, and made an appointment to see them that afternoon. I was not prepared to take the kids with me to the undertakers and the solicitors. I was finding it enough of a struggle. I just couldn't contend with them as well. I would have to rely on Sarah not to fall apart today, because I was definitely going to leave them here when I went out. And then fate came to my rescue. Andy walked in the door. Instead of snarling at me, he gave me a huge smile. I assumed that what he would have fancifully called a 'breakfast meeting' must have gone very well. I had no desire to discover what he was up to, but its obvious success was wonderful – for both of us.

Now or never, I thought. 'I have to see the undertakers and the solicitors. Any chance you could keep an eye on the kids?'

'Sure, no problem.'

I had a niggling feeling that one day the police would come looking for my brother, but as long as that wasn't today either... I gathered up the papers, along with my thoughts, and went back out to the garden. I heard Andy running upstairs; presumably he'd gone to put the mature look back in the wardrobe. The kids were sitting, side by side, on an old wooden bench.

'I've got to go. Andy's around, I think he'll be here for the rest of the day.'

'So, you're leaving us here, are you?'

My internal emotional flame flared. I extinguished it, with great difficulty. 'I'll see you later.'

Chapter 15

The undertaker had been very pleasant. I remember taking an instant dislike to the people who had arranged my parents' funeral, so this was a relief, but I really couldn't believe that his name was Bury! Perhaps some people were born to their professions.

I was also relieved to be able to leave the kids with Andy. I'd had enough problems answering a load of questions that I'd never thought would need answers, without having to cope with them too. No, I didn't have a favourite crematorium. That one looks fine; I don't really need the glossy brochure.

I was taking the decision totally on my own that cremation was acceptable. I didn't actually know. It wasn't something we had ever discussed. Perhaps Derek would have preferred a grave and a headstone, and a constant reminder that needed attention, and visiting and weeding! The will hadn't stated a preference, so selfishness pronounced that verdict.

No, I didn't have my own organist to play at the service, and I knew no vicars, whether from around here or not, and no, I didn't want a woman vicar. I have no idea where *that* reply came from!

No, there was no one who wanted to view the body. I was really glad the kids weren't there for *that* question. They hadn't asked to go back to the hospital to see him; perhaps they hadn't realized it was a possibility, and a huge cowardly streak in me had not suggested it.

No, I didn't want to go through to the back and look at various woods and linings and handles for coffins. The catalogue would do fine, thank you. I had said 'modest', remember?

No, I didn't want the hearse to go to his house first, or to my house, and one car would be plenty.

Yes, there would be flowers, or rather, I assumed there would. I suppose some people might prefer to give to a charity – I would have to think of an appropriate one. We'd have flowers, which would be at my home, but I would tell other people to send theirs here.

Yes, please send the bill to the solicitors, they are the executors. I prayed that that was right. I wasn't seeing them until later.

Yes, I would sort out the hymns I wanted the organist to play, and if I chose any music instead, I would bring an individual DVD for each piece – carefully labelled.

Yes, I would bring some clothes for Derek.

The ashes? I had no idea. Yes, just let me know when I could collect them.

I left in a daze, and in tears. Now, I didn't know what to do. The appointment with the solicitors was hours away. I could go to Derek's house, or I could go and find Sammy the paper man, or see if next door still lived there with her cat, but I simply couldn't deal with any of those. Or I could go home to the kids. I couldn't deal with that either. I drove on down the road, with no particular direction in mind. I had this very odd feeling that every car that came towards me knew where I'd been, and that I was trying to deal with the death of my boyfriend. My life had changed, and it felt as if everyone could recognize it in my face or my actions. I shook my head to try and clear it.

Suddenly I realized I had no idea where I was. The road was unfamiliar. It wasn't a tiny back street, but it certainly wasn't a main road either. There were no signs pointing to any places I knew. I saw a woman pushing a pram, but I couldn't make myself stop and say, 'Excuse me, where am I?' I reached a T-junction. Now what should I do? Left or right? A car went past me to the left, and I turned after it. A bend revealed some traffic lights and I prayed they'd turn red to give me a pause to think. They stayed resolutely green. The car in front went straight on. I followed. This wasn't a main road either. Traffic lights must mean I was near some sort of town, at least. There must be a sign soon, surely? This road didn't even have a shop in evidence. I glanced at the clock on the dashboard. Okay, I had plenty of time, but only if I could figure out where I was! Then the car in front signalled left and turned into the drive of a house. I panicked. I nearly followed it. I wanted to rush up to this unknown person and beg for help. Why had I left the kids at home? This was their neck of the woods; they might have known where I was.

I pulled over and stopped, and tried to take a few deep breaths. Just go back to the traffic lights, I told myself. It must be a main road; it must lead somewhere. I did a three-point turn that would have failed a driving test and headed back up the road. If the lights are green, I'll turn left, I told myself, if they're red... Then I saw the lights, and I wasn't allowed to turn right. Not having to make a choice was quite a relief, and then there were shops and a car park sign, and I felt myself relax a little. I was still lost, but at least this was civilization. A set of pedestrian lights gave me the pause I needed. The clock had only moved on six minutes, I still had hours to kill. I drove on. The road went upwards and over a bridge, and below me was the motorway. I made a decision. I drove to the coast.

Having parked somewhere that was going to cost me an arm and a leg for twenty minutes, I walked along the beach. A few people were in the sea, splashing around or throwing balls. Toddlers were building sandcastles with mums and dads. The sun was shining and there was a happy air about the place. I smiled back at a middle-aged man who had smiled at me, and briefly visualized him as a caricature of the typical English holidaymaker, sitting in his deckchair with a knotted handkerchief on his head. But I still felt as if I was wearing a sign saying, 'Recently bereaved. Do not approach.'

Eventually, I returned to the car, took off my shoes and emptied out the sand. It would only take about half an hour to get back to the solicitors, so I still had a good hour to use up. I started the car and pulled away, avoiding the motorway. That would have made the journey too quick.

I passed a pub that looked quite pleasant, so I pulled in. I was actually hungry. I didn't enjoy going into pubs alone, but the car park wasn't full, and it had an old-world charm about it that made it look okay. There was one elderly couple in a corner, and an even older man perched on a stool at the end of the bar. It was a lovely warm day, so I imagined that everyone else was in the gardens.

'Yes please?' the barman said. He had a heavy accent, mid-European.

'Pint of lager, please,' I answered, pointing to my choice from the various draughts on offer.

He looked slightly surprised. Maybe single women didn't drink pints in his part of the world, but they definitely did in mine.

'Do you do sandwiches?'

I paid and sat at a table in the window. Quite quickly, a young girl appeared with my sandwich. I smiled my thanks and then I was left alone, to have my lunch and contemplate the future.

Inevitably, I contemplated for too long. The drive back to Derek's home town brought on another panic attack. What if I couldn't park? Would they still see me if I wasn't on time? I didn't even know all the things I was supposed to be asking, and what happened if they wanted answers to things I didn't know? It was bad enough to be late, but I'd be arriving smelling of alcohol and I had no peppermints in the car. At that moment what I wanted most was another dose of alcohol, to deaden my emotions.

Actually, that wasn't quite true. What I wanted most was to turn the clock back.

Chapter 16

'So what did the solicitors say?'

I'd just related, to Phil, everything I could remember the undertaker saying, and I was beginning to feel as drained as yesterday. I rubbed my hands over my face.

'I'm sure I've forgotten half of what we discussed. I know he said that the undertaker's bill could go straight to them, but he said so much that a load of it went over my head. I think it's okay for the rugby club to send the bill for the reception to them, but I'm not totally certain, I'm sorry.'

He shrugged. 'Okay, we'll try that and see what happens. If it doesn't work, we can arrange something.'

'But it might be ages!'

'I don't think we'll go bankrupt.' He smiled at me. 'What happens about the kids?'

I sighed. 'He said it was unusual to have made a will without naming anyone as guardian for them, in case of, well, in case of *this*. But I guess Derek didn't know who to name.'

'Maybe he should have put the grandparents down.'

I snorted. 'Logically, maybe, but apparently the kids would now be old enough to fight against that, anyway.'

'So, what now?'

'Well, the house gets sold and the whole estate is divided equally between them. It's all in trusts until they're old enough. I don't think they'll have any money problems.'

'That's not what I meant.'

I glanced across at him. 'No, I know. I need to contact social services.'

He waited for a few moments, presumably to see if I'd add to that, but I think he could see the strain telling. 'Okay. If you want to talk, give me a shout.'

I nodded my thanks and he got to his feet and left me to sit and think. I had a lot to think about. I finished my mug of tea and went to make another. Looking through the kitchen window, I could see both kids at the far end of the garden. I'd insisted they went out, while I talked to Phil. I hoped they'd stay there too.

There were flashbacks of the conversation with the solicitor that I recalled with total clarity. At one point I'd had a feeling that he was wondering why I hadn't been named as guardian in the will. He probably wasn't, but my defensiveness had reared instantaneously, and I had told him, rather haughtily, that Derek had written his will when his wife had died, and that I hadn't even met him until years later! In that moment of anger I couldn't decide if he might be questioning my suitability to look after kids, or implying that I might have caused a rift between Derek and his wife that led to her suicide, or neither. Not that I was in any position to feel aggrieved that anyone should think I might have been having an extramarital affair.

It was immediately after that that he said I needed to contact social services, as the kids were now orphans and no one had parental responsibility for them. I was still feeling irritated and I may well have missed some of his next comments. I know he said that if they were ill, or had to go to hospital, no one had any rights to authorize treatment for them. He also said that a social worker would have to come and talk to all three of us. They'd want to know what the kids wanted, and what I wanted, as well. At some point he'd mentioned the possibility of foster care and I remember thinking, Good, that'll get them off my hands.

I stood up and looked through the window again. They were standing side by side, with their backs to me. I think they were watching a pair of squirrels in a tree – anything to try to take their minds off life as it was now.

'I hope the social worker talks to us separately,' I said to myself. I couldn't let them hear I'd be happy for someone else to look after them. I didn't want them to hate me. But perhaps I should wait, anyway, until I'd made contact with Derek's brother. He was family, after all. On that basis, maybe I should even talk to the grandparents first. I needed to form my own opinion about them, not just rely on what I'd heard. Maybe it would be doing the kids an injustice if I rushed to get a social worker here and force a decision straightaway. I didn't want responsibility for them, but I could at least be human about it. This was a tough time for all of us, and they did need my help at the moment. I guess they deserved that, at least. They'd just have to recognize the fact that I couldn't always be pleasant with it!

I moved away from the window. Now I really was going to have to start making all those sad phone calls. I walked slowly down the garden to tell Sarah and Tony. If they didn't want to hear me say, dozens of times, that their father had died, then it would be better if they stayed where they were.

I sat down and went through the address books to make sure I wasn't going to call the same person twice, and at the back of one I found a scribbled entry that just said, 'James', followed by a number. It began with 0061. I checked the phone book and found that it was the code for Australia. There was nothing else; no address or any indication if this was home or work. Derek and his brother obviously didn't write to each other. If they communicated at all, I guessed it was by email, and that was probably on his computer at work. I wondered how many other people would only be traceable that way. I certainly wasn't going to go to his office and sort that out. I may end up getting hold of all the wrong people and none of the right ones, but I would just have to ask people to pass on the news. I hoped that in the time I'd known him, if he had any bosom buddies that needed to be told, I would have heard about them.

I had no idea what time it was in Australia, but I dialled the number anyway. It was an answerphone. I left a message, explaining who I was and asking James to call me back. I didn't say why; no doubt I didn't need to. A call from his brother's girlfriend, out of the blue, was unlikely to be good news.

By the time I reached the bottom of my list I was very tearful. It wasn't so much what I was saying, as I'd developed a repeat script for my announcement and had somehow managed to stop listening to my own words, but the various reactions and the nice things people said about Derek really upset me. I walked out into the garden to get some fresh air. The kids had obviously been tearful too. Tony ran up to me for a hug, and they both followed me back inside for some lunch I didn't really want. We had barely finished eating when the phone started ringing. I imagined it would be callbacks from the messages I'd left, but it was work, and so were the next four calls.

'Stupid bloody woman!' I slammed down the phone, momentarily wondering if the client was still listening. 'Oh well, tough if she was,' I said aloud.

'Was what?' Tony asked.

I swung round, unaware he had been right behind me. Why I was surprised to find him there, I don't know; it seemed he'd been nowhere else for the past three days.

'Just forget I said anything.'

I didn't want a shadow, and having one was beginning to drive me nuts. I knew they were having a hard time, but so was I, and the added burden of two kids was making it a thousand times worse.

Sarah had just become very quiet, for long stretches. Even Andy couldn't pull her out of herself. If I stopped to consider what they were going through, I knew this must be pure hell for both of them, but I kept reminding myself that *actually* they were not my responsibility. Unfortunately, right now, that is exactly what they were. They probably needed to bawl their eyes out, with someone who was understanding and sympathetic, but at this moment that certainly wasn't me. I knew I was being completely and utterly selfish, but I really didn't want them here. I had never wanted them here, if I was honest. Hilary knew how little I was looking forward to them staying, in the first place, but they came as part of the package with Derek. The only reason they were acceptable was because Derek was there too, and they were *his* responsibility. Now I'd lost Derek and gained a millstone.

I poured myself a drink, choosing to ignore the fact that it was barely past three o'clock in the afternoon. I sat down in the lounge and Tony sat down beside me. I came closer to screaming at him than I had done for days, but the phone rang again, and I swore at that instead. I snatched up the receiver and snapped, '*What*?'

'May I speak to Alison Sheldon, please?'

I took a deep breath. If this is someone wanting a room decorated, I thought to myself, I'll probably suggest they stuff their head in the paste bucket. 'Speaking,' I replied curtly.

It wasn't a client; it was the doctor I had seen at the hospital.

At the end of the call, I had calmed down and my eyes were beginning to fill up with tears. Tony was watching me, and, for a moment, I felt sorry for him. He was eleven years old, he desperately wanted me to like him, and now he wanted to help me, but he didn't know what to do.

'Where's Sarah?' I asked him.

'Upstairs, I think.'

'Can you go and get her?'

He nodded and left. He would have done anything I asked him, even if I'd said go and jump off the roof, and I didn't want that responsibility either.

Before either of the kids returned, the front door opened. Phil poked his head into the room.

'You know exactly when to turn up, don't you?' I said, and got to my feet.

He gave me a big hug. 'How's it going?'

'I've just had the post-mortem report. Can you stay here a minute, while I tell the kids?'

'Of course I can.'

Tony reappeared, running, followed a few minutes later by Sarah. She looked tired and very depressed. I wasn't surprised, but maybe it was the first time I had really noticed what this was doing to her. For a second or two, I wished that it had been Andy who had arrived. Part of me knew that they both needed a great big hug too, but I couldn't give it to them. I was trying to hold myself together, trying to organize things that shouldn't have been down to me to organize, and getting absolutely nowhere with my own thoughts on what to do with these two. If I hugged Sarah now, it would be me that fell apart, and I feared I would also be inviting her into the rest of my life, and I knew that was what scared me most.

She sat down. Tony had already climbed as close to me as he could on the sofa. The whole scene was unreal. The awkwardness was tangible. I wanted to scream. I wanted to scream at them that it could well have been me that killed their father, by taking him on the squash court every week.

Instead, I took a large gulp of my drink and said, 'That was the hospital on the phone. Your dad apparently had a serious heart condition, which was what killed him. Obviously, he had no idea. Had he known, then probably something could have been done. All the physical exercise he took, and any kind of stress, has been threatening to do this for years. Because he didn't know, and had no treatment, this has been something just waiting to happen. The doctor was actually surprised it hadn't happened a long time ago.' I looked from Tony to Sarah. 'I'm sorry,' I added.

Sarah stared at me, and then the middle-aged child, who could so instantly bring out hostility in me, replied, 'He *should* have known. It was the same with *his* father.'

She never knew how close I came to slapping her. The only thing that stopped me was knowing that it would have been Derek that I was hitting. Very slowly, I stood up and moved towards the patio doors. I sensed Tony get up behind me and turned to face him. 'Just stay in here,' I said. I opened the doors and walked into the garden.

I don't know how long I would have sat there. I heard the telephone ring twice, but fortunately no one came to say it was for me. Suddenly I was aware of a presence beside me. Anger welled up and I turned very slowly, and very deliberately, to tell Tony to fuck off and leave me alone.

I have marvelled since at the power of nature to help in the most extreme of circumstances. I found myself staring into a sad-looking pair of eyes, but they didn't belong to Tony. I gazed back at the trusting, dejected animal in front of me, and carefully stood up, making as little movement as possible. Slowly, I walked back towards the house and leaned inside the door. The scene hadn't changed.

'Phil,' I said quietly, 'Sam's back, and she's hurt. Get some food, will you?' I looked at the kids. 'This is the fox we told you about. You can come and see her, but be very slow. She's been injured and she trusts us. Any violent movement will scare her, and she can't run right now. I think she's broken her leg.'

Tony suddenly developed the insight of his sister. He didn't jump up, he simply sat, motionless, where he was and said, 'Can I tell my friends it was an aardvark?'

I watched Sarah feed the injured fox. I watched Tony, by his sister's side for a change, desperately wanting to do it instead, and I looked at my big brother.

'You can't blame yourself, Ally, for Derek – or Sam!'

'But if I'd known...'

'Well, maybe Derek knew and chose not to accept it.'

'But why didn't he get checked out?'

'Some people can't face the answers.'

'But if his father had a problem, he only had to go and have some tests!' I stared at Phil in exasperation. 'What makes people hide from something they can cure?'

'Not wanting to know? Fear? Come on, Ally, you know it happens. Whatever the reason, it is *not* your fault.'

'But all the squash games!'

'He chose to play.'

'Do you think I'm ever going to accept that?'

137

He gave me a sad smile. 'You have to. You didn't kill him.'

'And will the kids accept that?'

'Probably sooner than you will.'

The phone rang again and I turned away with a snort of exasperation. Phil picked it up. 'Er…who's calling?' He held it out to me. 'Jim Lee.'

'Oh my God,' I muttered quietly, 'it's Derek's brother.'

Chapter 17

I hadn't woken up alone on a Sunday morning for quite a long time. The awful feeling in the pit of my stomach returned, a feeling of emptiness that somehow seemed to reflect my life. Not far away, along the cleverly altered first floor landing that I now couldn't care less about, were two kids who had never been so alone in their lives.

They weren't my responsibility, I told myself, and they certainly didn't have to be my responsibility in the future; but right now they were – maybe not legally, but morally. There wasn't anyone else who was panicking about them. No one else was aware of their situation. I knew I should have come home from the solicitors and immediately put in a call to social services, but I had succeeded in convincing myself that I needed to talk to Derek's brother first, and even, whatever the kids thought, to their grandparents. And I needed time to think. I told myself, in my own defence, that they were together and they were safe with me; I could wait a few days. They had a roof over their heads and they were being fed. I was the only one panicking.

I should have been lazing in Derek's bed, while he prepared breakfast, or letting him do the lazing while I went downstairs. I couldn't lay there any longer; sleep wasn't going to return. So I got up and went downstairs to prepare Sunday morning breakfast alone. Part of me wanted to call the kids and cook them breakfast. Part of me wanted to make them a substitute for what should have been. They needed help, and they certainly needed my affection, but if I'd called them it would not have been to give, it would have been to take.

I shouldn't have bothered about the emotions; both of them were already there. 'Hello.'

'Can I make you some coffee?' Sarah asked.

'Tea for me, thank you. I'll cook some breakfast. Scrambled eggs all right?' Derek always preferred his eggs scrambled.

'Yes, please,' the ever-hungry eleven-year-old answered.

His sister was more reticent. 'Not for me, thank you.'

It was all very polite. Glancing round, I realized that they had already had toast and something. Sarah must have noticed me looking. 'I'll wash the plates up as soon as I've made the tea.'

'Don't worry about it, I'll load the dishwasher later.'

I cooked the eggs as Derek and I liked them and gave Tony his plate. He peered down at it with a look of horror, as if he'd just been presented with something raw. Just as I noticed Sarah frown at him with a slight shake of the head, he started to cry. I rushed round to him and gave him a hug. For him or for me, I don't know.

'Dad liked them like that,' Sarah said. 'Tony likes his food done to death.' It was a bad choice of words, and it left a horrible silence.

I couldn't say what I wanted to say: Sundays will never be the same again; now there's another hole in my life that will have weekly reminders. Nor could I say what they needed to hear: It will get better, eventually. And I couldn't say, I'll cook some more eggs, as you like them.

I couldn't deal with this. I wanted to run away again.

Sarah ate the eggs. She may have hated them as well, but she ate them anyway. I knew Tony would still be hungry, but I chose to ignore it.

Phil appeared. His attempts at looking decent had lasted only the first week. He was in boxer shorts. Sarah looked down studiously, as if either she was embarrassed, or thought he would be. All I could think was that it was only last Sunday. How our worlds had changed since then. He grunted a vague greeting, made two cups of coffee and disappeared without further communication. From my point of view that was completely normal, but the two kids watched him go with bemused expressions.

'Have we done something wrong?' Tony looked like he was about to cry again.

'No, he just wouldn't have noticed you were here.'

'Like acceptance?' Sarah said.

I didn't reply, or even look at her. How could this child wind me up quite so much? After a very long pause, I got up, with my tea, and left the room. I think that Tony hadn't figured out if he'd had an answer to whether or not they had done something wrong, so he didn't follow me. The sun was up and I went and sat in the garden.

I hadn't figured out if I'd had any answers to the questions I'd been asking myself, so I knew how Tony felt. He was easy to deal with, in one way. He was an eleven-year-old lad.

He'd been protected by someone all his life. When he'd lost his mum, he still had his dad. Now he'd lost his dad, but he still had his sister – or me! His school was a protected environment. He wasn't shorter than average, or taller, or fatter. He was, so Derek had said, quite bright, without being a nerd, and he was well coordinated and very sporty, without being a show-off. He wasn't bullied. He was exactly what you saw in him, with no pretensions. He was still young enough to accept a hug, and young enough to show he needed one.

Sarah was altogether different. She'd grown up too quickly – she'd had to. I was sure that she needed a hug, far more desperately than her little brother, but she couldn't show it in the same uncomplicated way. She was a teenage girl, and that, by default, made her far more devious. I knew that, I'd been there. My guess was that she was hurting a hell of a lot more than I was.

Deep down, I really liked her, and I think she liked me, but we were now playing games with each other, and neither of us was going to submit first. She was probably very afraid of the future. She had lost the most important people in her life, and there was no one left to show her the affection she needed. Without doubt, she needed a mother, and she hadn't had one for a lot longer than just the time her mother had been dead. Maybe, had Derek and I gone on happily as a pair for the next umpteen years, she might have started to look to me as a substitute, but it would have taken time, and to make it worse – for her – I was absolutely certain that she knew I didn't want to be a mother.

There was no 'probably' about me being afraid of the future. I was.

It was a mess. She undoubtedly needed me, but she couldn't let herself show it; maybe she couldn't even admit it to herself, because there had to be a terrible fear of being abandoned by someone else. I wanted to help, but didn't want the responsibility that that would bring with it. Both of us may well have known how the other felt, and neither of us had the courage to voice those feelings. The worst part was that it would probably continue like this until one of us cracked, one way or another. Sarah would be fine one minute, then try and play the guilt card the next. I would help until I felt trapped, then I'd back off with a display of bad temper and selfishness. Maybe I could carry on, without doing anything highly regrettable, until they went back to school, but would that be the end of it?

That was the decision I couldn't face.

I had to get them – and me – through the funeral first, and then what? Did they just pack up a load of clothes and get dumped at the school gates, while I ran away from even thinking about their next holiday? Did they need new stuff for the next term? Derek had talked about Tony's football camp and Sarah having days away with her friends. What the hell should I do about all that?

I still had to deal with my own loss, and a funeral, and a gig in a week's time.

'Oh, just let me get through the next week,' I muttered to the heavens.

Decisions would have to be made, but I couldn't deal with any of them today. I stared down the garden and wondered idly if Hilary might fancy becoming a surrogate mother. At least that made me smile.

I stood up, took a deep breath, and went back inside, ready for the next round of the battle.

Chapter 18

'Where are you going?'

I looked round to see Tony standing in the hall, still in pyjamas.

'I'm going to work.'

'Can I come with you?'

'No, Tony, I've got dozens of things to sort out, and I haven't been there for days, remember?'

I saw his eyes begin to fill up and I swallowed, hard, to prevent mine from doing the same. It would have been easy to take him, but I needed to be away from them. I needed to be with Mark.

'Sarah will be here, you'll be okay with her.'

At that moment, his sister appeared and repeated her brother's question, only her tone was more aggressive. 'Where are you going?'

'To work,' I replied, again trying to keep the annoyance out of my voice.

'Do you have to?'

I stared at her, for a moment, and dismissed the first few replies that shot into my head. Finally I said, 'Actually, yes, I do have to.'

'And what are we supposed to do?'

'Sarah, I have no idea. I didn't wish for this situation any more than you. I'm trying to sort things out the best I can, and that includes figuring out an answer to what you're supposed to do.'

'Are you going to send us away?' Tony asked, anxiously.

'I don't know what I'm going to do.' I stared from one to the other. 'Perhaps your uncle will have some better ideas than me; he's arriving soon.'

'We don't know him,' Sarah said.

'Neither do I. But as your father neglected to cover this eventuality in his will, let's hope he spoke to someone else about it, other than your mother!'

It was the meanest of parting remarks, but my temper was getting very frayed. Sarah seemed intent on forcing me into a corner at every opportunity. I slammed the front door and hurried to my car, in case I was suddenly called back or followed.

Maybe it wasn't Sarah forcing me into a corner, maybe it was just my own fears. Every remark that seemed to require an answer about their future, however tenuous the connection, instantly filled me with alarm. Sarah's question may have carried no deeper meaning than how they should fill up their day, but I had read it as a challenge, a demand for my commitment. *I* was certain I was making them feel more and more afraid of the future. I was terrified about it. I should have gone back and apologized for my comment, but that might have led to me making a commitment, so I didn't. Had I snapped something exceedingly unkind at Phil or Andy – or vice versa – it would have been forgotten by the next time we met. But these two didn't have the security of affection that my brothers and I shared.

Derek's will had left them financial security, but no one specific to care for them. The solicitor had said that guardianship would undoubtedly have been discussed, but it must have been a nightmare for him. If he'd had any notion that he might have the same heart problem as his father, the turmoil would have been even worse. He couldn't put the grandparents down. I imagine he would have detested the thought of that as much as the kids did. I'd never met them, but from what I'd heard...

Derek's brother was another option, but where the hell was he? Yes, he lived in Australia, and was currently on his way to England, but other than that I knew very little about him, except that he probably wanted the responsibility of two kids about as much as I did, and the kids themselves barely remembered him. I supposed that making the will was the crucial thing, initially; naming a guardian could be done at a later stage. I guess he'd hoped they would be adults by the time he died. That brought more than a few tears to my eyes.

I was just turning out onto the road, when a thought struck me like a sledgehammer. Maybe Derek had decided exactly who he wanted to look after his children. Maybe that was precisely what this summer was all about, only he hadn't quite got round to asking me! I found that notion very disturbing. He hadn't said anything to me, but maybe he had to other people; his brother, for instance, or his friends, or even his wife's parents. He hadn't asked, and I hadn't agreed, but what kind of moral dilemma would it create if I found out that was what his intentions had been? And just what would I have replied if the question had been asked? But I knew that. It would have been no. It was still no.

*

I arrived at the house we were decorating, only vaguely aware of how I got there. Seeing Mark's van outside sent a flood of relief through me. I rang the bell and he answered the door almost immediately. Neither of us would have cared if the owners were in and wanting to talk to me; he just wrapped both arms round me and we stood there, in a silent embrace, for ages. Eventually we moved apart and, still without a word, he walked into their kitchen and switched the kettle on.

The owners were in, at least the wife was. She appeared in the doorway and simply said, 'Alison'. She gave my arm a squeeze and started to walk away again, then paused. 'Mark's doing a great job,' she said.

I nodded my thanks, unable to say anything.

He handed me a cup of tea. 'How are you doing?'

'I'm not sure.'

'And the kids?'

'They seem to be surviving, but I don't know what to do about them.' Suddenly I felt very tired and flopped onto a convenient chair. 'I'm not that much of a bitch to just call social services, or whoever, and get them off my hands, but perhaps that's what I *should* do. The grandparents are really responsible, they're next of kin, but they've made no offers. In fact, they barely said anything when I told them what had happened. I don't even know if they'll come to the funeral.

They're probably sitting at home, right now, dreading a call to say that two kids are being dumped on them.' I looked up at him. 'I can't have them, Mark, I can't!'

He didn't reply; there wasn't much he could say.

I finished my tea and went on. 'I don't want them to be deeply unhappy, which is why I haven't even broached the subject of the grandparents with them. I know they don't get on. I'd go so far as to say that Sarah hates them. Derek's brother is coming over for the funeral, but the kids hardly know him. I doubt that he's going to want anything to do with them, but maybe he'll have a better idea of what to do.'

Mark stood looking at me. 'When do they go back to school?'

'Oh, I don't know, it's about another six weeks, I think.'

'Well, unless you do dump them on the grandparents, or call social services, you're stuck with them for that time, at least.'

I stared at him. I had really done my best not to dwell too much on the time beyond the funeral. That was still three days away; because of the post-mortem, we hadn't been able to arrange a date before then. As it turned out, the post-mortem had been carried out quite quickly, and part of me was still smarting at this unnecessary delay.

'I guess you didn't want to hear that,' Mark said.

I shook my head. 'I've just put off thinking about it.'

'But even when they go back to school, that's not the end of it, is it?'

'No, it isn't.'

'Do you want to look after them?'

'I'm quite sure I don't.'

He let out a half-laugh, with little humour in it. 'And you know as well as I do, that when anyone says they're sure about something, it means that they're not!'

I rarely snapped at Mark, but I came close to it then. I didn't, because I knew he was right, and I found that frightening. I felt dazed and I felt trapped. 'What the hell am I going to do?'

'Right now, you don't need to be at work. I think you ought to go home.'

'I don't want to, it doesn't feel like home. Anyway, we need to sort the work out, for the next few days, at least.'

'I can manage here. We don't need to start at the Smithsons' straightaway; they'll understand.'

'I'm not going sit at home playing nursemaid right up to the funeral.' This time I did snap.

'No, but what you need to do is sit at home, alone, or go to Hilary's, and take some time for yourself. Ally, your boyfriend just died; this is not just about his kids. They're stopping you grieving for you. They're in the way. If you're coming to work to help *you*, then that's fine, but if you're coming here to escape from them, it's not fine. You'll make it through the funeral, and maybe even to the end of the summer holidays, and then you'll fall apart because you've buried your own emotions. You need to talk to someone about how *you* feel, not what to do with two brats!'

I gave him a weak smile. 'I was rather nasty to them before I came out, but I did come out for me. I came out to talk to you.'

'Then that's good. Come upstairs and paste some wallpaper for me and we can talk all day.'

'Let's have another cup of tea first?'

He smiled and filled the kettle. 'You know, each person has a unique way of dealing with things,' he said, with his back to me. 'When my dad died, I spent the evening singing myself hoarse in a karaoke pub. My friends and family thought I'd gone completely mad, but I needed to drink too much and scream.'

I remembered the charades.

He still hadn't turned round to look at me, but I knew he was telling me that it was okay to do whatever I needed to do. I picked up my mobile and dialled.

'Jane, it's Ally. I'll pick you up at seven for rehearsal, as usual.'

I looked up and saw Mark smiling at me.

It was amazing that two whole bedroom walls got papered. It was more amazing that the pattern matched perfectly and not one bubble was in evidence. Inevitably, as soon as we had gone into work mode, Mark relinquished any responsibility for hanging the wallpaper. He returned to his normal 'assistant' role and picked up the pasting brush, while I hung the paper. Neither of us had said anything, it's just the way it always was. He was perfectly capable without me, but when I was there, I took over. If I'd thought about it, it probably drove him mad. Nevertheless, by mid-afternoon, I'd had enough.

I wiped the paste off a joint and flung the sponge back in the bucket. 'Now I *am* going home.'

'Okay. See you when I see you.'

I nodded and he came across and gave me another long hug. 'Sing well tonight.'

I left the house with a little trace of a smile. I doubted that going out for a band rehearsal was going to be appreciated, but, excuse or not, Mark was right and I needed to go. Maybe it was simply to talk to Jane or, more particularly, to Kris, or maybe it was just to make life feel normal, or maybe it was to escape from Sarah and Tony... The reasons didn't matter, I was going.

I expected an element of annoyance when I announced I was out that night, but I didn't expect to be dealt a huge dose of emotional blackmail as soon as I walked in. Tony raced up to me and grabbed hold of me before I had even closed the door.

'I thought you weren't coming back,' he mumbled from somewhere in my shoulder.

I barely had time to catch my breath, before Sarah looked out from the lounge and informed me, 'He hasn't stopped crying all day. He was convinced you'd left us.'

I peeled Tony off me and dropped my bag on the floor. 'This is where I live,' I replied, somewhat unkindly, while regretted saying I'd collect Jane. A drink would have gone down quite well right now. I dismissed all the nice things I thought I might say, like, I hope you've been okay, and, What have you done today? Instead, I headed towards the kitchen, two shadows in tow, and said, 'I hope salad's all right for a meal, only I have to go out to a band rehearsal.'

'Can we come and hear you?'

I swung round and opened my mouth to tell Tony something I would probably have regretted for a long time, but was saved by Andy wandering into the room. 'Nope,' he replied for me. 'No one hears them rehearse. Even if they practise here, the rest of us are banned.'

I think Sarah was about to say something that I undoubtedly didn't want to hear, but Andy went on. 'The vicar called. Tomorrow at 11.30 is fine.'

'Okay, thanks.' I took a deep breath and looked at Sarah. 'You've got until then to try and remember if your dad had any favourite hymns.'

'Couldn't you play at the funeral?' Sarah suggested.

I looked at the wall, without replying, trying to decide if she had a very nasty, sarcastic streak or was simply being naive. Considering her often uncanny perceptiveness, I instantly ruled out naivety. 'I hardly think that anything I play would class as a favourite piece of his. *He* never heard us rehearse either!'

'He went to one of your concerts,' Sarah answered, defiantly.

I took a deeper breath, aware that I could suddenly hear my heart pounding in my ears, then turned round, very deliberately and walked across to her. I stopped about an arm's length from her face.

'Your dad didn't like country music. That's what we sing. He came to see me on stage, but not because he adored the musical content. Before you continue trying to make me feel bad about going out, or about anything else I've done, or haven't done, just remember one thing: you are not the only people who have lost someone in your lives, and we all have lives to get on with. We have to do it in our own ways. Don't push me too far, because you are not my responsibility. Carry on like this and I will pass you on to someone else, very rapidly. I am going out, and I will probably be back tonight, because, as I said before, I live here. Don't make assumptions that *you* do on a permanent basis!'

I left the house quite determined that I wouldn't be back that night. I often stayed at Jane's after practice, even when it was my turn to drive, and I never phoned home to tell anyone. Andy might be a bit peeved, but he wouldn't be surprised. Besides, if he was due to go out, go out he would. I would have dumped my problems on Andy, and he would simply dump them on Phil. If Phil didn't come home, so be it. That's the way we were. That's the way things happened in the house. Sibling number one left some mess for sibling number two, which they, in turn, left for number three. We might have a brief row about it the following day, but it was never that crucial; besides, the next time it happened, someone else would be number three! Perhaps two rather dependent, grieving children was a bit more of a mess than something like the fact that we'd run out of milk, but I decided the principle was the same. I knew I was making excuses, but, at that moment in time, I didn't care a bit.

I had been with them for days and, apart from my extremely rapid departure with Hilary one evening, I'd done my best to help them through this. No, I hadn't always been the most pleasant and understanding person, and I couldn't show them the affection they undoubtedly wanted, but, basically, I had been there. Today, for the first time, I'd spent the whole day away from them, and their reaction had entirely exhausted what compassion I had left.

I knew that it was only another excuse, but I did need to go out this evening – just for me. Mark was right.

Chapter 19

A huge part of me wanted this day never to dawn. It was almost inevitable then, that the day began for me, way before dawn broke. I lay awake in the dark, with a million thoughts assaulting my brain. I had attended quite a few funerals, but never before had I lost a contemporary. My parents' funeral had been the most difficult I could remember because, obviously, they had been the closest people I had lost before now. It had been extremely hard, but I had had my brothers with me. I knew that they would be there today, as well, but this was different; they weren't affected in the same way. But the kids would be. Sarah and Tony would look to me for support, but I had no one to lean on in the way I needed.

I would also have the problem of Derek's in-laws – if they appeared. The kids obviously didn't like them, and I had no idea what would transpire when they all came face to face. Perhaps they would arrive expecting to take their grandchildren home with them. No, they hadn't made any noises to indicate that that was their intention. But what if it happened? Could I bring the part of me that wanted the youngsters off my hands to the fore, and watch calmly while they were dragged off against their will? Supposing they *did* expect to take them, would it be because they felt responsible or even welcomed the responsibility? Or might it be because the kids had suddenly become potentially worth something in terms of a possible inheritance?

Then there was Derek's brother. He had seemed pleasant enough, when we had finally met, the previous night, but he wasn't someone with whom I felt any kind of rapport. Sarah had seemed very wary of him and Tony couldn't remember ever having seen him. He certainly didn't appear to have any interest in their welfare, or have the faintest idea what Derek's intentions about their future had been. I had got the distinct impression that attending his brother's funeral had been little more than an excuse to revisit England and catch up with some old mates. I wondered, if he had come over for some other reason, whether he and Derek would even have met up. He had consumed vast quantities of beer, and had seemingly assumed he was staying with me and did not have to find any accommodation for himself. No doubt, I would have offered, but I was a little irritated at the assumption. And how long was he expecting to stay? I asked myself.

Then there was me, and how I would cope with the day. I had suggested reading a short poem at the cremation service. Something had made me pluck it from a distant memory as a favourite of Derek's, but now I wasn't sure. I was also very unsure about reciting it. At that moment I couldn't even remember the first line. I had asked Sarah if she wanted to say something, but she'd shaken her head. She would probably regret that later, but I'd given her no further chance to change her mind.

I hadn't much liked the vicar either. As I lay there, watching the first traces of daylight creeping up, I began to doubt that he would remember what I'd said to him about

Derek. He hadn't written anything down and obviously he never knew him.

I'd picked out three hymns, without any consultation with the kids. What if I'd picked some that they knew he hated? Then, of course, there was one huge aspect that I hadn't even considered. Derek and I had never really talked about religion. The most I knew was that he put C of E on forms. He may actually have been a total atheist, or violently anti-religion, and no more than a conformist when it came to anything official. I may have organized something that would have offended him. I may have arranged a service that would have his friends rolling around in the aisles in disbelief.

And what about his friends? I hardly knew them. I'd only met two or three, and then only briefly. I'd spoken to everyone I found in his address book, but no one had given me any insight into what sort of service I should arrange. But then, I hadn't asked them, so they would all assume that I knew everything there was to know about Derek. It might become patently obvious this afternoon that, actually, I didn't know him at all. This whole day could be a total disaster.

*

I had taken the kids back to Derek's after I'd spoken to the vicar. It was probably the hardest journey we'd made. How do you decide what clothes are suitable to have someone you care about cremated in? We had found some appropriate outfits for the kids to wear to the funeral, although neither seemed too enthusiastic about what had been, essentially, my choice. Perhaps I should have let them wear whatever they wanted, and not suggested that it should, at least, be sombre. We had then delivered Derek's clothes to the undertakers. When we arrived, they both seemed to panic and refused to come inside with me. Maybe they'd thought they would see their dad lying in there.

Phil had got his rugby club, where we were going for drinks afterwards, to organize some food. It wasn't too far from the crematorium and it was vaguely halfway between my house and Derek's, as Hilary had pointed out. I had thought Phil was an angel from heaven when he'd agreed to sort it all out. I was so relieved not to have my home full of strangers after the service. Also, I could run away and go home if it got too bad. Sarah had seemed almost shocked that we were going to a sports club. I hadn't yet discovered if it was too frivolous for her or if, perhaps, she felt it was bad taste, as it might have been excessive sport that had killed her dad. She had also found it odd that the coffin was going straight to the crematorium and not from the house.

I climbed reluctantly out of bed. 'But this is *my* house, not his,' I muttered to myself. 'And when did she become such an expert on funeral etiquette anyway?' I went downstairs with mixed emotions. I wanted to be alone, but didn't. I wanted to have someone put a cup of tea in my hand, but not have to speak. I found a cold, empty kitchen. It stayed cold, but it wasn't empty for long.

Tony had probably been awake as long as me, and was only waiting to hear movement. When he appeared, his face seemed to be a mixture of relief that it was me and not someone else and fear of how I would treat him. I extended an arm and he ran eagerly to wrap himself in it.

'Tea?'

'Yes, please.'

'I'm not cooking; you can get yourself some cereal.'

'Okay.'

Maybe he was learning how to treat me. He clearly wanted to stay attached, but moved away. He obviously wanted to talk, but remained silent. He probably wanted to cry, but then so did I.

Gradually the kitchen filled up, but there was little conversation. There was an unusual air of politeness. People apologized if they bumped into each other. I recalled this atmosphere from some years previously; but then there had been three of us remembering our parents. I think today we were back there again.

People left the kitchen and reappeared, dressed and ready to go. I wandered around the garden and discovered I'd remembered the poem. Andy arrived by my side and put a glass in my hand and I found it was midday. We stood silently, staring at the plants, until Phil came to join us.

'The car's here.'

I spotted Hilary outside, putting flowers in the boot with the driver and pointing out which bouquet was the main one. She gave me a nod, but made no move to come and speak to me. Any display of compassion would finish me off, and I had to get through the poem, at least. I ushered the kids towards the car. Hilary climbed in with us, as did Andy. I looked round, in a moment of panic, for Phil.

'He's driving his car,' Andy said. 'The car will only take us to the club; someone needs to bring us home.'

'Oh, yes, of course.' But actually I had wanted my big brother there beside me. James seated himself next to the driver.

The silent journey seemed to take forever.

*

The hearse was waiting at the beginning of the drive. All heads turned slowly, in unison, to look at it, as we drove sedately past. It moved in behind us for the final few metres of the journey. There appeared to be a lot of people as we stopped by the crematorium doors. I glanced across a mass of unfamiliar faces. Beyond my own friends, I only recognized two or three, and then I saw two more, standing slightly behind the others. I didn't need to be told they were Derek's in-laws. Sarah must have seen them at the same time, as I felt her tense up.

'It'll be all right,' I said quietly and squeezed her hand.

When we got out of the car I felt extremely awkward. There were so many people I didn't know, and yet I'd organized all this. I chose to ignore the in-laws at this stage; I knew I'd have to speak to them later. I nodded to my own friends, but kept away from them. I couldn't deal with their sympathy at that moment. I also felt I couldn't leave the kids. The vicar emerged and I used talking to him as an excuse not to mingle. A few friends and colleagues of Derek's introduced themselves, then suddenly we were being told to go inside. I took hold of Sarah and Tony's hands and we walked slowly to our seats.

The service was a blur. I vaguely remember the vicar saying something about Derek that wasn't quite right – I knew he hadn't been listening. People did their best to sing the hymns, but the organist had pitched them at boy-soprano level. And then I heard, 'Alison would like to read a poem and say a few words.'

My stomach lurched. I was only going to recite the poem; I wasn't going to say anything else! I walked as calmly as I could to the lectern, cleared my throat, which seemed very loud, and managed to recall all the words. After a momentary silence, I heard myself say, 'It's very sad for me to be meeting so many of you, for the first time, in such circumstances, but thank you all for coming. We will all miss Derek very much.'

I couldn't have said any more, even if I'd thought of something; my voice cracked on the final word. I walked back to my seat. I think the vicar said a prayer, and then suddenly the curtains were moving around the coffin and I was left with a brief glimpse of a brightly coloured bouquet of flowers that I knew bore a card that simply said: 'Dad, with all our love.'

James got to his feet and stood back to let me and the kids out first. I took their hands again and we walked outside into a bright, sunny afternoon.

'Let's go and look at your dad's flowers.'

They were lying on the ground, by a small plaque that bore his name. There weren't that many. I had given people an option of a donation to a heart disease-related charity, but I think some had given both. Sarah bent down to read the cards, but Tony wouldn't let go of my hand.

'What would you like to do with the flowers?' I asked her.

'Can we take them home?'

I nearly said to her, Do you mean my home or your home?, but they hadn't really got a home any more. 'Yes, of course we can. We'll find a nice place in the garden to put them, shall we?'

She stood up and took my hand again. After a moment she said, 'The flowers will die. Could we put something with them that won't?'

I had a momentary awful, guilt-ridden vision of some horrendous tombstone-type statue in my garden, and I hated myself. I hated myself so instantly that the tears started to roll down my face. I realized both of them were looking at me. I coughed, and swallowed. She might not even have been talking about my home.

'We'll go to the garden centre, and you two can choose a really nice shrub.'

'Thank you,' Sarah answered, quietly.

Hilary arrived beside me and I let go of the kids and received a big hug.

'Could you tell the driver we'd like to take the flowers?'

She nodded. 'I think the car's ready. Phil's leading a convoy back to the club.'

I still hadn't spoken to most people, but there was a whole afternoon to get through. We got back into the large black car and Andy leaned across to me. 'Your guitar's in Phil's boot.'

I smiled my thanks. It may not have been Derek's way, or probably the children's way either, but it was mine and my brothers'. There had to be singing at some stage. It gave us a release of emotion. The first time I ever attended a funeral, when I was quite young, I remember being slightly horrified when someone appeared with a banjo during the afternoon. It took less than five minutes for me to understand how it helped. We sang for hours after my parents were buried, and there was lots of laughter too; singing, laughter and loads and loads of great memories. I wanted this day to end the same way. I hoped that Sarah and Tony would understand.

I didn't really expect Derek's wife's parents to come back to the sports club. Or maybe that was simply a hope. Unfortunately, they were the first people we met as we walked into the room.

'You must be Alison.' The father extended a hand, quite formally. 'And how are you, Sarah?'

'I'm all right.'

'We're sorry for your loss.' He didn't wait for any further response from her before turning back to me. 'I'm not certain exactly when the children are due back at boarding school, but we go away this weekend for two weeks. Perhaps we can talk about arrangements when we return?'

We had all stopped in the doorway. Sarah was just staring up at them. Tony was almost hiding behind me. A dozen

164

things flashed through my mind. I wanted to say that he was an unfeeling bastard and no wonder his daughter had committed suicide, because she had clearly had no love from her parents. Instead I replied, 'What arrangements?'

'About the children and the property.' He sounded surprised that I needed to ask.

I took a deep breath. 'We are carrying out Derek's wishes, according to his will. I can make you aware of what his requests were, when you get back, if you wish.'

I fought down a huge urge to tell them that they did not figure, in *any* way, in the will. 'You have my number. Feel free to call me if you want to. Now, if you'll excuse me, I need to see to the other guests.' I glanced round. 'Sarah, Tony, let's go in.'

Tony was glued to me. He wasn't doing anything else but following me. I sensed Sarah's head rise a little. For a couple of moments, from her point of view, I was wonderful. I glanced back over my shoulder. 'Please help yourselves to drinks and something to eat.'

Hilary was suddenly beside me. I paused and let both kids walk on with Andy.

'Bloody hell!' she muttered. 'What a bastard!'

'My thoughts, exactly.'

'What are you going to do?'

'I really don't know. If I send them to those two, they'll probably end up doing the same as their mother! I really must talk to social services. And I must find out what happens if they decide they want to take the kids, because no way can I let that happen! I couldn't pack them off to those ghastly people, even if I wanted to.' I looked at her, with a feeling of desperation. 'They'll have to stay with me, won't they?'

'Is that what *you* want?'

'No, it isn't. It really isn't.'

'Well, it looks like you or foster parents.'

'And what happens if the foster parents turn out to be as awful as those two; after all, they were parents once!'

Hilary stared me full in the face. 'What are you saying?'

I couldn't hold her gaze and looked down at the floor. 'I don't know, Hilary, I don't know.'

Chapter 20

I have heard people say, on more than one occasion, that the day after a funeral is the worst day of all. The initial, numbing shock of the loss has subsided; all the frenetic rushing around to get things organized is over; and all the help from people calling in has come to an end. All that's left is the deep sadness, and a million things to sort out, each of which brings back its own memory. For me, there was all of that, and two kids!

Phil found me sitting in the garden, smoking. 'Have you made any decision about the kids, yet?'

'No, I haven't!' I snapped at him.

'James is on the phone, trying to arrange a trip to Manchester.'

'Right.'

'He'll be off as soon as he sorts it out.'

'Right.'

'I think he's trying for a train this afternoon. I suggested we all went to the pub for lunch.'

'Yes, okay. Where are the kids?'

'Andy took them out somewhere, in the car.'

I looked at him, in surprise. 'Oh.'

'They'll meet us in the pub.' Phil sat down. 'Look, Ally, Andy and I do need to know what's happening with them.'

'Are you telling me to throw them out?'

'Do you want them to live here?'

'No, I don't!'

'Then why are you having a go at me?'

I glared at him for moment, and then dropped my head. 'Sorry. I wish I had some miracle answer. No, I don't want the responsibility of them, and James certainly doesn't. I think he's made that quite clear with the way he's arranging all sorts of trips around the country. This is just a holiday to him. He's hardly likely to return to Australia with some ready-made family. From the few things that Derek ever said about him, I gather he's already walked out on one family. I think that's why he emigrated.' I lit yet another cigarette, stared at it, swore at myself and threw it across the lawn. 'And the grandparents are evil.'

'That's a little strong!'

'Maybe so, but at best they are not nice people. The kids don't like them at all, and anyway, they're going away and don't want to know anything till they come back. Even then, my guess is that their only interest is in the house and any money that might come their way. Maybe they think they have a right to some cash on behalf of their daughter.'

'I assume there's no boarding at their schools during the summer.'

I looked round at him. 'I don't think I could do *that* to them, quite so soon, even if there was.'

'So they're staying for now, anyway.'

'I guess they'll have to.'

'So, Andy and I need to know what's happening, as I said, in case you need our help.'

I flopped my head onto his shoulder. 'Sorry, I was being a right shit!'

'What's new?' he said, jumping up, in case I hit him.

I found a smile.

'Have you contacted social services?' he asked, from a safe distance.

'No, not yet!'

'Shouldn't you have done that by now?'

'Since when did you become the expert?'

'I didn't come out here for a fight. I'll shout when we're ready to leave.'

I was sure I should have contacted social services by now, but there was that niggling piece of knowledge that when I did, they were going to ask me what I wanted. But I knew I didn't want the kids here. So why didn't I just make the call and get rid of them? Maybe there are times when something deep inside stops you reaching in and finding the answers. Something tells you that you don't want to hear them. Yes, I would sit down at some stage and let myself *really* think about it. At some stage. When I was ready. I stood up, went inside, locked the doors and got ready to go out for a drink.

We returned from the pub, with barely enough time for James to collect his luggage before the taxi arrived. They weren't exactly fond farewells. Certainly he and I were never likely to visit each other again, and he offered no invitation for the kids to go to Australia at any point in the future. I sensed a great relief when he left, from both Sarah and Tony. I guess they were afraid, right up until that minute, that they would be packed up and sent off with him. Personally, I did not feel relief, just a gnawing doubt about the responsibility that seemed to increase from the moment of his departure.

The answerphone had been flashing three messages since we had come back from the funeral the day before, but we'd all ignored it. Recently, every message had been for me, and I certainly hadn't wanted to listen to anything last night. We had sung for a long time, then, quite late in the evening, I'd finally heard both kids starting to talk about great memories of their dad. I wasn't about to ruin it by playing some sad message from someone who couldn't make the funeral.

We walked back indoors as the taxi vanished from view. Andy stopped, looked at the phone, decided not to bother and ambled off somewhere else. I stabbed at the play button, hoping that one message was for him, which I'd subsequently forget to pass on... Then I remembered that he had been a great help. Old habits still lingered.

The first was some American voice telling us that we had won a holiday. The second was the sister of a neighbour of some person Mark and I had worked for months ago, who wanted a new bathroom fitted.

I wanted to go back to the pub, and I very nearly didn't play the third message. Reluctantly I pressed the button again. It was from Craig, with some panic about the interval set for the barn dance. Typical of him, I thought to myself, that he's forgotten he's phoning on the day of the funeral.

'Oh, my God!'

I said it so loudly, that not only did my persistent shadows both jump in fright, but both brothers reappeared in the hall.

'It's tomorrow!'

'What is?'

'The barn dance. The gig!'

If I had expected any kind of useful reply, I didn't get one.

'Jesus Christ!' I muttered, irreverently, and picked up the phone.

'Craig, it's me.'

I ended the call and raced up the stairs, leaving both kids staring after me. Having found my play list, I scribbled some vital alterations, then sat down heavily on the bed. If I got uptight before gigs, it was nothing compared to Craig. He still hadn't remembered it was the day of the funeral when he phoned, but two children downstairs probably couldn't believe how quickly I'd forgotten it. If *I'd* felt that awful 'morning after the funeral' feeling, how badly must it have hit them? I did have another life, which, right now, was very important to me, but they had nothing but each other...and me.

After resolving that giving up smoking again could wait until after tomorrow, I went back downstairs. They hadn't moved.

'Come on,' I said, with a deep sigh. 'You'll have to give me a hand sorting out some space. Your belongings have got to go somewhere.'

Tony only heard that we were bringing his stuff to my house, he looked pleased, and relieved. I think Sarah only heard my sigh. I ignored the look on her face and thought for a moment. 'Actually, maybe it would make more sense for us to drive down to the house and see what needs to be shifted. I don't know how much space we need.'

'That would be good, yes, thank you.'

I'd redeemed myself with Sarah.

I had dumped all the materials out of my car with Mark, so for once it was empty. There was loads of space to bring back loads of stuff. With that depressing thought, I picked up my bag, checked the cigarettes were still in there and told them we might as well go straightaway.

*

There seemed to be more of an air of sad acceptance about Sarah when we arrived, although she still looked on the point of tears. I didn't feel too great either. Tony was agitated. If Sarah was finding acceptance, he seemed to be becoming more insecure. He returned to hanging on to me, refusing to go inside without holding my hand. I wondered if he thought I might leave them there and run off.

We sat in the kitchen. It was a bright summer day, but the house felt cold. I hadn't thought to bring milk, so I couldn't make tea, but Sarah had found some Coke, which they were drinking. I declined. I hated the stuff.

'I think, from what I remember, that everything in the house will be sold and the money will go into the trusts set up for you.' I knew I should have listened more carefully to the solicitor. 'Obviously your personal stuff is yours, and we can take that with us, but if there's anything else specific you want to keep, you'd better tell me, and I'll try and find out how you can do that. I'm sorry, I don't know exactly how it all works.'

'What happens if we want to take something that belonged to all of us?'

'Well, if it's a memento of some kind, and isn't as large as, say, the piano, that might be worth something, I'd be inclined to suggest you just take it. If we get our knuckles rapped, I'm sure we can live with it.'

Tony smiled.

'Where will we live?' Sarah asked.

It was the question I'd been dreading.

'Until you go back to school, I think you'd better stay with me.'

'And after that?'

I took a long time before I gave them the only honest answer I could. 'I don't know.'

Sarah almost looked as if she admired my honesty. Tony looked bewildered.

'We have a million things to talk about, but what's important now is for you to decide what you want from here.'

I sent them off to their bedrooms, with a stern warning that I wasn't taking everything this time. I wondered how many more times we would have to come back and do this. I walked slowly round the house, touching things, thinking that everything I had come to find familiar would soon be gone. How on earth could these two deal with it? In a little over a year I had come to have my favourite bits of this house. To them, things like the piano had been there before they were born. I could walk away from it, because none of it had ever really been mine, but could they?

I came across a photo of Derek and me on a window ledge. I don't like having my picture taken, but this one was okay. It was in my hands when Sarah came into the room.

'May I take this?'

I think a few more years of maturity were added to her fifteen-going-on-fifty mentality at that moment.

'Yes, of course, thank you for asking. If there's anything else you'd like, let me know. Let's all get our knuckles rapped.'

I nodded my gratitude, with an attempt at a smile.

'I won't go to our grandparents,' she announced, 'and I won't let Tony go there either.'

I nodded again.

Having made her announcement, she returned upstairs.

I was aware of raised voices.

'No, Tony, you don't want it.'

'But I do!'

'Well, you're not going to able to take it, so just leave it alone.'

I almost smiled. We were about to have a childish tantrum. Instead, a heart-rending shout of anguished appeal for help came from Tony. 'Mum!'

As a moment's regression, from a hurt eleven-year-old, I wasn't certain if it would have been a worse reminder for all of us if he'd called for his dad. But then a sudden, awful realization hit me. It wasn't regression. He was calling to me.

Chapter 21

The remains of last night's takeaway were still in the kitchen. Curry smells before breakfast weren't my idea of a pleasant greeting. I threw the containers in the bin and got rid of the plates into the dishwasher. The smell remained. Having made a pint-sized mug of tea and grabbed some sort of cereal bar from the cupboard, I retreated from the fumes into the lounge. I was sitting, playing through a guitar part in my head when Sarah walked in. She started to say something and I jumped. I had actually forgotten they were in the house.

She realized she'd startled me. 'Sorry. Can I make us some breakfast?'

'Yes, sure, do what you want.'

I shook my head at myself. Hardly a compassionate greeting, I reflected. Tempering it, slightly, I called after her, 'The curry smell might have gone by now.'

She was out of view just long enough for me to refuse to dwell on the fact that I had totally eradicated them from my memory and force my mind back to the guitar part. Today was about me, and my gig. Inevitably, before long, they forced themselves back into my mind.

They must have eaten in the kitchen, with the curry, but now they had a whole day to get through, and I was there – available – in the lounge. Sarah's entry was fairly sedate, but Tony raced in and all but jumped onto the sofa beside me. He bumped into my left hand, as I was imitating a complex series of chord changes.

'Hey!' I snapped, pulling my hand away, as if he might harm what was, that day, my most valuable asset.

He looked suitably chastened.

Sarah said, 'We need to do some washing.'

If she'd spoken to me in a foreign language, I doubt I would have given her a more astounded look. After a full minute, I replied, 'I don't have time to deal with that today. I've got too much to sort out before tonight. Everything's in the utility room. Do you know how to use a washing machine?'

'Of course.'

'Okay. Then it's all yours. Hang things in the garden; don't put them on the radiators. They're not on, anyway.'

She walked away, pulling a reluctant brother with her.

Washing? I thought. Someone else's washing? I ran up the stairs and shut my bedroom door with a loud bang.

What they did for the next couple of hours, I have no idea. I soaked in a bath, my left hand hanging out of the water, so I didn't soften the necessary corns on the ends of my fingers, and ignored thoughts of children. I couldn't quite manage to return to the blissful state of having forgotten their existence, but the bath helped. By the time I reappeared, Phil and Kath were in the kitchen, and both kids were in the garden.

'What time does it all kick off tonight?'

'The barn dance starts at seven. We're meeting at five to set up the gear, then going to Jane's. We won't go back to the hall until just before the interval. That'll be about 8.30.'

'How come they're having a do like this on a Sunday?' Kath asked.

'It's Jane's sports club. She plays hockey there. It's their summer festival day. They have all sorts of hockey and football, and other games there in the afternoon, then a big buffet spread, followed by a barn dance. It's usually pretty good. This is the third year we've done it.'

'Is she playing hockey this afternoon?'

'Yes, sadly. That's always our biggest fear – broken fingers!'

Phil chuckled. 'She broke a fingernail last year, and the rest of them nearly murdered her.'

'Well, it was a crucial plucking nail!'

Phil got up to make some more tea and coffee just as the front door closed. We all peered out of the kitchen in curiosity. Andy was being followed in by the 5-series BMW owner. Our mouths fell open. Andy so rarely brought his dates home; this one must be serious. Mind you, I thought the one that got us up to look at a deer and created the aardvark rule was serious, and where was she now?

Andy ambled into the kitchen, as if he did this sort of thing every day. 'Kirstin, this is my brother, Phil, and my sister, Alison.' He swung round with his usual air of graciousness. 'Oh, and this is Kath, a friend of Phil's.'

She smiled that obscenely white, regular row of teeth at us. I hated her again, but only for a very short moment, because she suddenly focused on me and said, 'I'm really looking forward to this evening. Andy's told me all about the band and what you play.'

'Oh, thank you. It's okay if you can bear country music.'

'I love country music. It's so hard to find anywhere to hear it, these days. There used to be a radio station that played it, but they went out of existence. How do you manage to keep up with the current stuff?'

I think I was in danger of collapsing on the closest chair, but Sarah and Tony suddenly appeared. I guessed that they had seen Andy arrive. It was obvious, instantly, that Sarah certainly hadn't seen he had company. Her face fell. I suppose that, however little progress she might have made with any kind of romantic attachment, she had never actually seen him with a girlfriend before. Up until now, she could hang on to hope. That had just been shattered. Tony just looked a little shy as my brother introduced them to Kirstin. Andy had presumably given her the background on the kids, but she made no sympathetic comments. She also seemed to have forgotten she had an interest in country music and had been talking to me.

An awkward silence developed. It's probably not that easy to chat to a group of strangers that included two kids who had had their father cremated two days ago. Maybe something as trivial as music seemed inappropriate.

I had no interest in the answer, but asked Sarah, 'Did you get your washing sorted out?'

'Yes, thank you.'

Tony returned to my side and I gave him a quick hug. Someone had to scythe through this atmosphere, so I stood up. 'Come on, the pub's open.' I looked across at my elder brother. 'Can you squash three in the back of your car?'

'Yes, sure.'

I motioned for the kids to follow me.

Sarah was very quiet and seemed as upset as on Friday, although I doubted it was, at that precise moment, with memories of her dad.

It wasn't one of Andy's finest hours, but perhaps Sarah needed to see that her crush would go nowhere. Perhaps Andy needed to let her know that as well, for both their sakes. She wasn't getting a great deal of help from my family at the moment.

We sat in the gardens of the pub, in the sunshine, but it still wasn't a very bright day – emotionally. Conversation was sparse, and after a while Andy and Kirstin wandered off to look at the river that bordered the pub grounds. Sarah seemed to be almost on the verge of tears, and I couldn't cope with that today.

'Are you two hungry?' I asked them.

Tony, inevitably, was, but Sarah just shook her head.

I gave her hand a squeeze and raised my glass. 'To absent friends.'

We left Andy and the current love of his life in the pub, and went back home. I threw together some sandwiches and was about to disappear to sort out my gear for the evening, when a sudden bout of uncharacteristic compassion hit me.

'If you two would like to come and help set up the gear this afternoon, you can stick around with me till we go back to the club to play, but you'll have to come back home afterwards with Phil.' That part had already been arranged, as I would stay the night at Jane's. The rest I would have to break to the other three in the band and hope they accepted it.

Sarah almost smiled.

As a band, we were never going to be anything more than we were, but we loved it anyway. The practice sessions were an important part of our social lives, and we all recognized that the gigs were just the occasional carrot necessary to make us work. We probably played to an audience no more than three times a year, but it didn't really matter. The largest stage we'd stood on was in a school hall, but that didn't matter either. The only person who regretted this arrangement was Kris's dad. Given half a chance, he'd have booked us at the Albert Hall!

He attended every gig. He had been the one who first bought us any amplification equipment, as a birthday present for Kris. Talk about living your life through your children! His enthusiasm was infectious and even Kris had to admit he was useful. He was our roadie for the gigs. The sound equipment was stored at his house. It had started its life there, before Kris left home, and no one had the heart to take it away from him. He looked after it, helped us put it up and dismantle it. He drove us anywhere we needed to go for the gigs and took us back afterwards, which gave the four of us a chance to have a few drinks. Kris and I had laughingly speculated that maybe he did it to keep an eye on his little boy, in case he was seduced by one of the naughty girls in the band, although we had managed to get round that on a couple of occasions…

Kris also thought that his dad – Tom – set up our gear in his garage and played for himself, at times. He actually did a passable Hank Williams impression, given half a chance. None of us had a problem with that – we weren't so sure how his neighbours felt.

I drove myself, my guitar, a bag of clothes and two kids to the sports club. It was a quiet journey, during which I was dreading any questions about Andy and his girlfriend. Just as I pulled up and parked, Sarah said, 'Dad was looking forward to this evening.'

It caught me unawares, and I felt my eyes start to prickle. I couldn't cry now, I couldn't! I just nodded. Speaking might have let me down. Suddenly Tom was beside the car, grinning at me, and Derek Lee – deceased – left my thoughts in one selfish second.

It must have been well over half an hour later I realized that we'd lost Tony. Sarah had followed us around, at a safe distance. No one had asked her to do anything and she hadn't offered. Craig was in his usual manic state; Kris was ignoring him and Jane was out on a hockey field somewhere. Finally everything was set up, but we were now competing with the people organizing the buffet, trying to check sound levels. I approached one microphone and got a horrendous feedback shriek. It was only because Sarah let out a squeal of fright, as she was right beside a speaker, that I noticed her. Momentarily, responsibility flashed into my mind, as I looked around for her brother. It was rapidly followed by annoyance.

'Where's Tony?'

'I don't know.'

'Oh shit!' It was only a mumble, but I was right beside the now fully functioning microphone. A large cheer went up in response from a group of footballers, heading for the changing rooms. I grinned and gave them a flamboyant bow.

Sarah stood watching me, looking totally out of place. My entire insides flipped over. I was in my own world, one that was special to me, one in which I actually thrived. Hers had been destroyed, and the only person she had to rely on had forgotten where we had all been forty-eight hours ago. The buzz in me drained away.

'Are we all set?' I asked Tom.

He nodded happily.

'Okay, I'll see you at Jane's.'

At that moment Jane walked in, still carrying a hockey stick. 'Sorry guys, we got stuck with playing the final game. What's left to do?'

'Nothing, you lazy bugger!'

'Oh, I'm mortified!'

The men all laughed. Suddenly, I couldn't. I picked up my guitar and walked over to Sarah. 'I'll just put this in the car and we'll go and find Tony. He's probably watching the football.'

Silently, she followed me.

*

I parked outside Jane's house, took the guitar out carefully and ushered the kids through the gate. Both of them, now, were silent. We had found Tony watching a penalty shootout. He had got so caught up in it that he was genuinely keen to wait and watch the outcome, but as we approached he must have seen Sarah's face and his expression became instantly sober, if not guilt-ridden with the recognition that he had been enjoying himself. I didn't know what to say, so I hadn't said anything.

Just as we were reaching the door, a thought struck me. When my relationship with Rob had ended, it ended suddenly and totally unexpectedly. No, he hadn't died, but I'd had no more chance to have those last few, deeply necessary, words with him, than if he had. And his letter had all but killed me. I wrote a song about it, some weeks later, and balled my eyes out over it, for many, many weeks after that. One night at a rehearsal, something in my head had suddenly made me need to have this piece of desolate melancholy witnessed by my closest musical friends. I think I sang it with such feeling that their response to it was a stunned silence. After a full five minutes Kris said, 'Sing it again', and he had picked up his guitar and started humming a possible harmony, and Craig had joined in with a slow funereal slide of brushes on the snare drum. Then Jane had relinquished the comfort zone of her guitar for the more challenging one of her violin, and instantly created the most mournful introduction that, to me, summed up its entire mood. It was a performance piece that was created that night, in an instant. During the last year and a half we had added it to our repertoire. Now I could just about sing it without falling apart. It was in tonight's set. As I looked at the kids, the lyrics sprang into my head. I stopped walking.

'It's going to be a bit chaotic in here. We have to check everything we're doing, tune up, then we've all got to go and change. We'll sing a few bits, probably throw a few tantrums, and then it'll be time to leave. We'll all squash into Tom's van and when we get back to the sports club you'll have to find Phil or Hilary yourselves. I won't have time to find them for you.'

Two serious faces stared at me.

'But I want you to know that I wish your dad was here, and I'll be dedicating a song to him tonight. I won't say that on stage, but you'll know when you hear it. You just have to listen to the words.'

Sarah reached out and took my free hand, just for a second.

'Thank you,' she said

I wanted to hug her. Actually, I wanted her to hug me. Instead, I did my best to smile. Tony was easy to hug, he was a little kid, and he'd become more of a kid over the last week and a half. Sarah had become a grieving woman, but we could only touch hands; it was the most we'd done. The other grieving woman had to forget all about grief tonight. I swallowed hard and wondered whether I could actually get through that song tonight. Now it had a double meaning. With a deep breath, I rang the doorbell.

Chapter 22

Jane opened the door, still in her tracksuit, and stared at the two additions.

'Oh,' was her only reaction.

I had completely forgotten to tell the others they were coming with me.

Reactions did not improve, on moving inside. I have no idea if Tom was bothered, or not. His views carried no weight, anyway. Kris frowned deeply and Craig simply looked shocked. Probably, at that precise moment, he remembered that I had been at a funeral two days before and realized just who had died. He may also have remembered that his last call to me was actually on the day of the funeral.

The whole scene became a frozen tableau.

I just felt angry; angry with the kids for screwing up this evening, and very angry with myself for making such a stupid decision. What on earth had I been thinking? What had possessed to me to find compassion tonight? I needed to rescue this situation rapidly. I would have to deal with offending the kids later.

'I know, guys, I'm sorry, I should have said they were coming. It's just till we go back to the club. They are not going to get in the way. Could someone get me a drink, please? I'd like you all to raise a glass to Derek, and his children, and then simply forget they're here. This is our night. If I can deal with it, so can you.'

I turned back to two very uncomfortable-looking kids. 'I'm sorry; this isn't easy for any of us. There's not one person here who doesn't wish life was different, but we have to do this tonight, and this part - before the gig, takes all our concentration. You'll just have to sit here and keep quiet. I believe your dad would have understood.'

Whether Derek would have understood or not, I had no idea. I doubted that he would have been too enamoured about how I'd just spoken to his offspring, but I wasn't going to dwell on that. Someone put a glass in my hand and I discovered that Tom had found some Coke for the kids. He was the only parent present and his opinion of me had probably just hit rock bottom.

Kris lifted his beer can. 'To your dad, and to you.'

A quiet mumble reflected his toast. Craig tipped a large shot of what was probably vodka down his throat and leapt to his feet. It was typical that he was the one to recover the quickest. He could not stay calm before a gig; he needed to be back in manic mode or he couldn't play drums or sing. The rest of us needed that as well.

Within twenty minutes, it appeared that the rest of the band had followed my instructions and forgotten we had two orphans with us. I certainly had. Chunks of pizza were passed round; the conversation got louder and Craig stamped his foot – literally – on more than one occasion, as he was shouted down about a couple of suggested last-minute changes. We rehearsed one or two short passages from about three numbers, and talked over a few past performances, with some groans, and some occasionally quite graphic language. Then Kris insisted we practised the opening of the first song. He played a chord, and four voices let rip with the most horrendously discordant notes imaginable. We all collapsed in laughter and Craig said, 'Perfect!' Then we leapt up, disappeared to various other rooms and returned, giggling and wearing our cowboy hats. I doubted that Sarah could have equated what she and her brother had witnessed over the previous hour and a half with me telling them it needed all our concentration.

Instruments were picked up as if they were precious gems, and we went out to the van. Sarah and Tony were herded into the front seat beside Tom.

*

The sports club car park was full. We could hear the barn dance caller, as we approached and Tom pulled up to let us out. Both kids started to move, but he put a gentle hand on Sarah's shoulder and told them to stay with him. I glanced back at them as I climbed out.

'See you later.' Then I gave Tom a smile that I hope conveyed my thanks and my apologies for being such a bitch.

Jane led us in through the back of the men's changing rooms, and she and I started making cracks about whether we might be lucky and find some footballers still in the plunge bath. We found no naked men, but I began to feel that I was getting into the right frame of mind – at last.

None of these three had been to the funeral. I didn't ask them; I didn't want them there. My relationship with them was special, and it excluded others when we were together as a band. There was an understanding between us that only band members can appreciate. We relied on each other. We trusted each other. At times, we carried each other on stage, without even a glance. Disasters happened on stage, once in a while, but they never manifested themselves as disasters. Someone always managed to retrieve any situation. The audience never noticed, and any change always appeared seamless, or part of some comic section of the act. It wasn't rehearsed; it couldn't be. Had Derek died when we were months from the next gig, I think that all of them would have been there to support me on Friday, but it had been too close to tonight. I had a horrible feeling that I might need a bit more than the normal support and friendship from them this evening.

Rehearsals and performances had their set patterns; it had been the same for years, and part of the pattern for a gig had to include a lot of banter. If we had walked out on stage having had a deeply serious conversation, we would probably all have dried up.

'Shall we check the showers?' Jane asked.

'Is it worth it?'

'Well, there are a couple of new guys in the third eleven. You never know, there might be the odd aching muscle that needs a rub!'

'Next year,' Craig asked, 'can we come in through the women's changing rooms?'

We paused before the door, checked our tuning with ears clamped to guitars, against the background of taped barn dance music and a phoney American accent from the caller, and waited for our cue. We could hear that the place was jumping. It sounded fuller than ever. The dance ended with a round of applause, and gradually the voices became louder as everyone started to discuss their prowess – or lack of it – on the dance floor, and fight their way to the bar.

Craig was peering at his watch. He had decided he knew exactly how long it took everyone to calm down, get themselves a drink refill and find a seat. For the rest of us, we knew that when the conversation buzz started to subside, it was the right time.

The noise dropped a few decibels, and Jane, Kris and I exchanged glances. Craig lifted his head from his watch and said, 'Now.' His three compatriots snorted with laughter.

We slid inside into a shadow. I was aware that a few people, closest to us, had witnessed our arrival, but not the vast majority. Quietly, we picked up leads and plugged them into the pickups on our acoustic guitars. Craig picked up his sticks and twirled them ostentatiously through his fingers. It was a good sign.

'We are okay,' I said to myself.

He hit three gentle beats, Kris hit a chord, and four voices in perfect four-part harmony, hit one hell of an opening note. The lights glared on, the hall went totally silent, and that amazing creepy feeling crawled up my back and across my head.

God, I loved this!

We completed the set with 'El Paso'. It went quite well. The guitar part was perfect, but my concentration on it made me forget to sing a few 'hums' as harmony once or twice, but I doubt anyone noticed but me. My final 'twiddle' – as Craig always called it – was drowned out by some very serious applause. Without anyone having suggested it, we all took off our hats and gave the audience a deep bow. By the time we had unplugged the guitars and stored them carefully, a crowd of familiar faces had arrived near the stage.

'They love you!' Tom said.

'That probably means there are more people this year that don't want to go back to the dancing!'

But it did feel as if they liked us.

We gratefully grabbed the pints of beer and lager that Tom was carrying, and looked around to see who was there. I spotted both brothers with respective other halves, Hilary, four other friends and, slightly behind the others, two kids. They would have to wait. I briefly joined my friends. We didn't have that long before the dancing restarted, and it was too early to relax. We had another set. I received a couple of inquiries about how I was doing, but my friends knew better than to talk much to me now. We slipped back into the changing rooms and prepared to sit out the next hour, and indulge in a bit more banter.

The time passed quickly. Tom brought a tray of drink refills; we checked a few points for the next songs; Craig told us two very long and awful jokes and then the prolonged applause was signalling the end of the dancing.

This time, when we emerged, there was quite a lot of clapping. That was a good sign. We started, as we usually did, with three up-tempo numbers, with no pause between them. By the end of those, we'd competed favourably with glasses being refilled and recaptured our audience.

I stepped forward to the microphone. Something made me look round the hall, and I caught Sarah's eye. Jane's soulful violin introduction started and I took a deep breath and sang the first line.

'You never gave me a chance to say goodbye...'

I usually repeated the last line, but this time I couldn't. I'm not even sure that I stepped away from the mike to give them any indication. The other three simply played the final few notes as naturally as if there never had been an extra line.

The next two songs were a blur. I tipped my hat forward a bit, grateful for its cover, and by the time I had to be more in evidence, I was back in control. I thanked God, not for the first time that night.

We played two encores, and I think we were all beginning to wonder what would happen if we needed a third, but Tom solved that dilemma by turning up the main hall lights. We waved our hats vigorously and vanished into the changing rooms. Now we could relax. There were lots of whoops and hugs and back-slapping and loud, excited voices.

'Come on,' Craig said, 'I need a drink, and, of course, to meet our adoring public.'

Suddenly I felt drained. 'Thanks, guys.'

Craig grinned, winked at me, punched the air and vanished out through the doors. One day he would say something sympathetic and the three of us would die of shock, but if any one of us really needed help, we all knew he would be the first one there. Jane gave me a look that said, We can talk about this all night, if you need to. Kris squeezed my shoulder. God alone knew how special these three were. I closed my eyes for a moment, and tried to let the usual feeling that followed a gig take its effect, but it just wasn't quite there on this occasion. I breathed in deeply, made myself raise my head and followed the others into the main hall.

We all had friends there and we drifted off towards different groups of people. Hilary had a pint of lager in her hand for me, which I seized gratefully. One skiing friend of mine, Pete, who had been to the funeral on Friday, came up and gave me a massive bear hug. 'You did brilliantly tonight,' he said, and I started to cry.

I should have been on a high, with music still buzzing in my head, but I cried instead. Pete wouldn't let go of me, and eventually I had to fight my way from his grasp in order to have another large gulp of lager.

I found Sarah standing in front of me. She had tears in her eyes too. Hesitantly, she moved forward, and, very tentatively, for the first time, I gave her a hug.

Chapter 23

I arrived back home feeling distinctly bleary-eyed. At least I didn't have a headache. I hadn't quite managed to match the mood of the others last night, but I'd gone drink for drink with them anyway. Jane and I must have fallen into bed at about three o'clock, but the lads and Tom still had a drive after that. I dreaded to think how they felt this morning.

It had taken an age to dismantle all the gear, even with Tom's help. As usual, it was Craig's drum kit that took the longest. He kept threatening to add at least one more drum, if not two, to the ensemble. We constantly told him how great he sounded with what he'd got! Then we had to go through the ritual of Craig making Tom promise faithfully to lock the van in the garage overnight, talk through his entire security procedure and arrange a precise time that he would be round to collect his drums, before we could get into the serious drinking.

My head might have been spared pain, but I was dehydrated enough to want gallons of tea. I dumped my stuff in the hall – the delicate treatment not quite as important as the night before – and headed into the kitchen. Both kids were there and they started to applaud.

I laughed. 'Thank you.'

'It was really cool last night! Can I have your autograph?'

'You certainly can. Would you like coffee?'

'You're all very good,' Sarah said.

'Thank you, again.'

'And the song was wonderful.'

I just nodded, with a sad smile, thinking, Please don't ask me anything about it. I didn't think I'd mentioned that I wrote it, so hopefully she couldn't ask me if it was about anyone. She didn't. What she did say, though, surprised me.

'Tony, would you go away, please.'

'What?'

'Go back to what you were doing.'

'I wasn't doing anything!'

'Well, just go back to where you were earlier, for five minutes.'

He left with a dark look at his sister.

'Could I talk to you for a minute?'

'Sure,' I replied through held breath, trying to continue, nonchalantly, to make tea and coffee, and wondering what the hell was coming now!

'I need to do some shopping.' She hesitated. 'I need some things from the chemist.'

'Oh! Oh, right. If it's an emergency, you can have a look in my bathroom cabinet.'

'It's not for right now,' she went on, not looking at me. 'Dad used to give me some money and drop me at the shops.'

My heart went out to her. How long had it been since she'd had a mum? She'd probably had to go through the trauma of her first period alone.

'Would you rather do that? I can drop you at the shops this morning.'

She nodded gratefully.

No doubt she could talk to her friends about it without a second thought, but I wasn't a friend of her own age, and I wasn't the mum she hadn't had when she'd needed one.

'I guess we'd better have a think about shopping in general,' I said. I don't know what else you need, either of you.'

'Nothing much, right now, but we will before we go back to school.'

That brought me back to earth with a bump. How long away was that? And then I thought about money. I would have to pay for this. How much did they want? Was there a great long list of things for the next term? Would I ever get reimbursed? Just as I was telling myself what a selfish cow I was being, Tony reappeared. He'd obviously decided that five minutes was up and he might be missing something. Putting my self-centred thoughts aside, I winked at Sarah. She managed a slightly embarrassed smile.

Tony looked from one to the other, as if to see if anyone was going to enlighten him, then sat back down at the table, still looking sulky.

Suddenly a thought hit me, and my sharp intake of breath made both of them look up. Without doubt, it was only selfish reasons that had given me the thought, but I'd returned from the hospital with a bag full of Derek's belongings and put them in the study. They were still there, presumably including his wallet. God, I hated myself sometimes. Money aside, they needed sorting out and I wasn't looking forward to going through more of his personal effects.

'There's something we need to do,' I said.

We all cried a little staring at the things spread out on the table. The enclosed list, from the hospital, was very detailed and very impersonal. It was the list that finished me off, before I even saw what it referred to. Item seven was: Plastic rose. He'd probably bought it for me as a joke, just like the one he'd left on the pillow at his house. We weren't going to be there for weeks, so he'd got a substitute for my pillow at home. I couldn't read any further. My eyes filled up and I put the paper aside, through a blur. Both kids were watching me; they hadn't touched anything.

There were the wash things, clean socks and shirt that I had taken in for him, and a spare pair of boxer shorts to sleep in. Derek didn't do pyjamas. The worn socks and shorts were in a separate bag, with his shirt. I wasn't going to open that any more than was necessary to check the contents. I imagined the shirt was bloodstained. His other clothes were there, and his keys.

Christ! I'd done nothing about the car! I vaguely remembered the lout at the hospital telling me it had been taken somewhere, but I'd done nothing about it! Was it still there? Were there things of Derek's in it? Was it even drivable? It was nearly two weeks ago. They might have destroyed it.

Suddenly Phil walked into the kitchen. I'd forgotten he'd broken up from school, and he made me jump. Before he had a chance to speak, I gabbled all sorts of things about cars and garage yards, and hospitals and belongings, just grateful to have someone to talk at.

He probably made little sense of most of what I said – I was hardly speaking calmly – but he saw the things on the table, and registered the tearful faces and the car keys in my hand.

'I'll find out,' he said, and walked back out of the room.

Very, very grateful for an elder brother, I tried to calm down again and go back to sorting through the other things; his watch, his wallet, some loose change, the copper bracelet he wore and, of course, the plastic rose. I picked up the rose and held it in my hands, while I tried to recall if he'd had anything else with him when he'd gone out that morning, in case it was still in the car, but then I remembered, I hadn't seen him go. If they hadn't been in front of me on the kitchen table, I wouldn't even have known what he was wearing.

And still the kids hadn't touched anything.

I pushed the wallet towards Sarah. 'You'd better go through that.' Then I picked up the watch and glanced at her. She read my mind and nodded.

'I think this is yours now, Tony.'

He didn't know whether to smile or cry. Eventually he did both, as he put the oversized watch on his wrist.

Sarah carefully took all the contents from the wallet, one by one.

'The credit cards and bank card need to be cut up. Do you want me to do it?'

She nodded.

We ended up with cards, driving licence and insurance certificate, a library ticket, membership of the RSPB, a few scraps of paper with numbers on, one credit card slip and £170.

'The money is yours,' I said. 'I should probably declare it to the solicitor, but what the hell? Just divide it between you.'

Sarah looked at it for a long time, and then said, 'You take a hundred, because you're paying for us at the moment, and we'll have the rest for the other things we need to buy.'

I swallowed very hard. I felt very selfish, again.

She pushed five twenty-pound notes towards me. I saw Tony watching a potential fifty pounds of pocket money disappearing across the table. He wasn't being selfish; he was just being eleven.

Ten minutes before, I'd simply have pocketed it, now I couldn't. I got up and fetched a small wooden box that Phil or Andy had made in their youth, which sat on the window sill. 'I tell you what, we'll put it in here for emergencies.'

Phil came back in. 'I've located the car, it's a write-off, I'm afraid. Nothing's been done to it. We'll need the insurance details so they can assess it, and then that money becomes part of the estate. If you want to see if there's anything in it, you can go today. I'll run you down there, if you like; we'll take the insurance stuff with us.'

Then I remembered he'd had to do this before. I got up and we gave each other a long hug.

Phil moved away and put the kettle on. He'd probably been gasping for coffee when he first appeared and I'd hijacked him. I sat down and Sarah silently handed me the credit card slip. I didn't even notice the amount, just the heading at the top.

After a very long pause I said, 'Tony?'

He looked up from examining his watch.

'What date was the boat booked for?'

I think that, foolishly, I expected a simple, albeit sad, answer to my question, but his face lit up. 'Can we still go?'

Chapter 24

At first glance, the car looked just as I'd last seen it. The passenger side was totally unblemished. My wonderful brother went into the office to sort out the paperwork. I certainly didn't want to hear too many details. Three of us were left staring at the car. I took one of their hands in each of mine and we walked towards it. He'd obviously been hit from the side. The front wing was almost non-existent. The wheel hung at a distorted angle and the damage extended into the engine and back through a large part of the driving door. God, it must have been a shock, when it happened. The other car must have been going at quite a lick. I found myself praying that it hadn't been Derek's fault.

We stood in silence, looking at it, probably each of us visualizing him in there. I walked back to the passenger side and tried the door; it was open. There was very little inside: a road map and a few sweet papers that I assumed were Tony's were on the floor, and nothing more than the handbook was in the glove compartment. The boot catch was stiff, but it opened. His briefcase was in there, and his golf shoes. In my mind I saw his clubs sitting in my utility room. He'd unpacked those, but left the shoes. The briefcase wasn't locked and seemed to contain some work-related papers. I supposed that his firm would want them. There was nothing else; no emotional shocks, thank God, but nothing personal or frivolous either. There were no furry dice, nodding dogs or stickers on the window.

I took out the shoes and the case, and closed the boot. Phil was already in his car, waiting for us, and we drove home without a word. He would pick the right time to tell me anything else he'd found out about the accident. I thought about asking him to stop, to let Sarah go shopping, but it wouldn't have been fair on her.

*

Conversations about boat trips had been curtailed – to my immense relief – by Phil coming in and suggesting we went to the car yard. I could really have done with him invading our space when we got back to the house, but he announced he was off somewhere, and did no more than let us out of the car before driving off.

With a weight on my shoulders that felt as if it was rising by a kilo per minute, I opened the door. 'We need to talk about boats,' I began, as soon as we were inside.

I sensed Tony's instant eagerness. I thought, We need to talk about the fact that they are cramped, uncomfortable, slippery, dangerous and ultimately very boring. What I said instead was, 'So, I suggest that I drive us all to the pub, fittingly by the river, to have some lunch and discuss it.'

I picked up my car keys. 'We are also going to stop on the way, because Sarah wants to get some odds and ends from the shops, so you, Tony, can give me your opinion while she's gone.'

It was the closest thing to a conspiratorial grin that I'd received from Sarah.

I pulled into the car park. 'There's the supermarket, obviously; there's a chemist next door, then a flower shop and the book shop is over the road.'

'What does she want?' Tony asked, as his sister got out of the car.

'I have no idea. Do you want anything?'

He shook his head, then said, 'I want to go on a boat.'

I would probably have little more than ten minutes for this conversation, I thought to myself. I really had to use it wisely.

'What is so special about going on a boat?'

'I've never been on one.'

'Okay, that may be true, but this was supposed to be a holiday for you, Sarah and your dad.'

'And it would have been the first one!'

I completely lost any ability to stay calm and remain in control of the conversation. 'You mean that you've never had a summer holiday since your mum died?'

'No, not a real one. We meant to, every year, but something always happened, and we couldn't.'

The frenetic discussion between Derek and these two about holidays instantly flashed back into mind. No wonder no one cared where they were going. No wonder no one listened to anyone else.

Oh, Derek, why didn't you ever tell me?

I was almost afraid to ask. 'When was the last time you went away for a real summer holiday?'

'I think I was six,' he said matter-of-factly. 'We had a caravan in Wittering, or something.'

I couldn't think of a single thing to say, but it was Tony who continued, and it all but destroyed me.

'It's hard to go back to school and everyone says, where did you go on holiday?'

There was such innocence in his comment. There was no blame, it was just the way it had been, and it broke my heart. I was still sitting in some sort of state of shock when Sarah came back to the car.

'Did you get what you needed?' I forced myself to ask.

'Yes, thanks.'

'What did you want?' Tony asked.

'A revision book for maths.'

I don't know if she had the excuse ready, or whether I gave her the idea by mentioning the bookshop. It made me smile, at least.

I bought them orange juices and sandwiches and we sat out in the pub gardens. My pint of lager vanished before I'd had a mouthful of food. I told myself I could drive on two pints and bought another before I even contemplated starting a conversation I would probably regret for the rest of my days.

'I know Tony still wants to go on the boat. How about you, Sarah?'

She didn't answer straightaway and I knew I simply had to dive in.

'I think I've just begun to understand what summer holidays mean. No, it won't be anything like how special it would have been if your dad was with you. It can never be like going away with Mum and Dad, as most of us were lucky enough to do as kids. But it would be a summer holiday. I am not your mum, no one can replace her – or your dad – but I can take you away for a holiday, and at least you can laugh about it with your mates when you get back.'

'Wow! Cool!' Tony said.

Sarah stood up. 'I'd just like to go and look at the river.' I think she wanted to cry.

Tony started talking excitedly about boats as if everything was decided.

'Hold on, Sarah hasn't made up her mind yet.'

'But she always wants to go as well!'

'I know, but this wouldn't be the same. This wouldn't be what you've both been looking forward to. It can't be. Your dad's not here any more.'

He hung his head and fiddled with the watch. He had the strap as tight as it would go, but it still kept slipping over his hand.

I hoped Sarah would hurry back, because I wanted another drink and I would have to go home for that.

She finally returned, and it was obvious she had been crying. 'It would be very nice of you, thank you.'

Tony beamed.

'Well, there are a few practicalities to discuss,' I said, thinking, A few? 'So let's go home and talk about it.'

I drove them back, knowing that the first thing I had to do – after getting another beer – was to phone Hilary. She would think I needed certifying!

*

Hilary didn't burst out laughing. She went very quiet and then said, 'God, Ally, are you sure you know what you're doing?'

I was suddenly fairly certain that I didn't. 'Wouldn't like to join us, would you?'

She sighed. 'Sorry, I can't help this time. I'm off to San Francisco next week, remember? And I have to say, I'm not sure I'd come with you, even if I could.'

I didn't reply and she went on.

'You'd better make up your mind if you do want to become a substitute mother, because this is going to seem like one giant step towards it.'

'Perhaps I could find a crowd of mates to come as well?'

'When is this boat booked for?'

'The day after tomorrow.'

'Then it's very unlikely. I expect everyone's already made plans, but anyway, the kids will still look to you as the parent figure, however large a support group you try to wrap round yourself.'

'Yes, you're right,' I said soberly. 'Do you know, they haven't had a summer holiday since their mum died?'

I heard her let out a breath. 'I thought Derek took them away in the summer?'

'So did I. Apparently something at work always screwed it up and it never happened. I had just worked out a way of putting Tony off boats, and convincing him that a holiday without their dad would only be a sad reminder, when he came out with that! Something inside me just said I'd got to do it. I think I was really mad with Derek, as well.'

She was quiet for a while. 'I'm still not sure you're doing the right thing, but I probably would have done the same.'

'I may have to phone you every day!'

She laughed slightly. 'Okay, I'll try not to say I told you so every time!'

'Which day are you flying out?'

'Wednesday.'

'Oh,' I groaned slightly. That was the day we were due to complete the boat trip, and I would have dearly loved to know I could see Hilary before her holiday and, more especially, *after* mine.

We ended the call and I thought to myself, What have I done? I walked slowly into the lounge, where Tony – predictably – was pouring over the boating brochure.

Perhaps, more to the point, I continued questioning myself, Why have I done it?

Chapter 25

When Derek had gone to book the boat, it was just for some time in the future. All I'd remembered was that it was a mid-week start and after the gig, which took precedence, and I had about two weeks to talk myself out of it. Now the only thought I had was that it was the last thing he had done for his children before he died. The huge irony was that, with their track record of holidays not coming to fruition, I may not have had to talk myself out of it at all. Something could have cropped up with Derek's job, as it obviously had in so many previous years. Then they would have been back to odd days out somewhere. Why on earth hadn't I decided to take the days out option instead?

I had just felt so sorry for them. Now I felt sorry for me.

Mark had been very surprised when I told him I was going, but we had already vaguely covered the eventuality of me not being at work for a week, although I don't think either of us had really believed it would happen. I knew he could cope, and my mobile phone would never be anywhere but attached to me, in case he needed to call, and we would only be on a river that was less than ten miles away.

I had gone into the travel agent's alone and explained the whole sad story of why our holiday numbers had changed, and managed to swap the large flashy boat that Tony was so keen on to something smaller and definitely less powerful. He would have a sulk, but it would be short-lived. I think all the staff were nearly in tears by the time I left. I know *I* was fighting it. I had even achieved a cash refund on the difference, which was more than likely not allowed, but, of course, Derek's credit card account had been closed, so I couldn't give it to them to swipe through. It hadn't been my intention. I hadn't even thought of the price difference, but it was useful. They had phoned the boatyard and been reassured that one adult and two kids could handle this boat, and, yes, we would have a training session before they let us go.

Packing had been a nightmare! I refused to go through Tony's bag item by item; I simply told him what he needed and then sent him back upstairs – twice – to take at least half of the contents out! Then I had sat them down for the conversation I needed to have and they didn't want to hear.

'First, I need to say that this holiday may not work.'

'Why?'

'Well, it happens sometimes that people don't get along, or things don't work out, or even that the weather is a disaster.'

'But it's sunny!' I knew Tony would have counter-arguments to everything I said, but I had to make my point. I was also trying to forget that the only time I had had a holiday where people didn't get along was with a group of friends from college – on a boat! We had had at least two blazing rows, and one of the guys had simply walked off.

'What I'm saying is that any of the three of us could decide they don't like the holiday, and if that happens we can come home at any time. If it's not working, we *will* come home.'

Sarah nodded and Tony looked sulky, but I had my let-out clause.

'Also, boats are slippery and dangerous, and it's easy to fall in.'

'We can both swim.'

'Not if you're knocked out, you can't! If I tell you to do something, or not do something, I'm not saying it to spoil your fun. I want us all to be safe.'

Well, I thought to myself, I'm certainly *sounding* like a parent!

We stopped on the way to the boat yard for provisions. I couldn't believe how much they felt was necessary. I wasn't sure the boat cupboards would be big enough. I finally heaved the trolley to the checkout. I had gone in to cater for breakfasts and lunches for about three days, knowing we would probably eat at waterside pubs in the evenings. I hadn't allowed for snacks: vast amounts of biscuits, crisps, chocolate, sweets, Coke and lemonade.

I had almost completed transferring everything to some ten carrier bags, and was at the point of getting the exorbitant total, when Tony suddenly said, 'Oh, I forgot the mints,' and ran off.

I opened my mouth to say something, but he'd gone. The cashier smiled at me and I shook my head with a sigh. He reappeared and announced to her that we were going on a boat.

'I think your mum's going to make you walk the plank!' she told him.

I didn't say anything, but he gave me a huge grin and said, 'Sorry, *Mum*!'

When he'd called that out four days before it had filled me with apprehension. Now his cheeky grin made it amusing. There was no instant twinge of fear this time. I reflected on that briefly as I gathered up the bags. Well, he had only said it as a joke…

*

'Okay,' the yard owner said, 'Who's ever handled a boat?' He was probably not as old as he looked. His skin was like crinkled leather, tanned and ruined by years of being in the sun.

'These two haven't,' I told him, 'and I'm certain that this young man wants to learn how to steer, as well as just about every other detail about how the engine and everything else works.'

We all obediently donned life jackets, although I knew mine would be off as soon as we were out of sight of the yard. Tony looked as if all his Christmases had come at once, as he was allowed to take the boat away from its moorings and up the river. He was even allowed to turn it round, with a bit of assistance. Actually he was quite good.

The boat man pushed the throttle to neutral and said, 'Okay, let your sister have a go now.'

'I don't want to drive, thanks.'

Momentarily I wondered if this was connected to driving cars and what happened to her dad. In case that was true, and to prevent any questions, I offered to take it back. I was quite proud of how I took it into the mooring, and the yard owner stepped off very easily.

'Throw me the back rope, young lady.' Sarah tossed it straight into his hands and looked rather pleased with herself.

We somehow managed to stack the food; it was our clothes that ended up without much space. I looked at the map and decided how far we would go that day. However long this holiday lasted, we weren't very likely to get to the end of the navigable waterway, so there was no point making it a race. There were plenty of mooring places marked, so having chosen a suitable target that took us through no locks on day one, I told the kids to untie a rope each and step back on board. The man gave the bow a shove, gave us a wave and we were away on our holiday. And I had more than a fleeting memory of saying to myself that worrying about kids falling off boats was not my scene at all!

We chugged along at a nice sedate pace, and even Tony didn't seem to care that we weren't in a speed boat. He did want to sit on the bow, but I refused to let him. Just before he drove me mad going from one end of the boat to another to investigate everything, I realized that the only way to stop him fidgeting was to give him the wheel. Whether I'd ever let him take it onto a mooring, I doubted, but it kept him quiet and gave me a chance to get out of my life jacket with a stern, 'Don't do as I do, do as I say.'

We hadn't travelled a massive distance when we found ourselves approaching a small island in the river. Two boats were moored to the island on the main stream side, but nothing was behind it against the bank. It looked ideal, so I dispatched Sarah to grab the front rope and wait to jump off as we touched the bank. I took the wheel from Tony, much to his disgust, and sent him aft to throw the other rope. We hadn't practised this, of course.

I was so determined to get the boat close to the bank, at less than walking pace, that I managed to all but envelop Sarah in an overhanging tree. She did laugh, and she fought her way out and stepped ashore. I revved the throttle briefly in reverse, and shouted at her to tie the rope to a mooring post. It all looked very expert as she did that, and walked back to receive the aft rope from Tony. He threw it, but no-one had told him how to coil a rope properly, when we'd first pulled away, and instead of flying freely towards his sister, it fell in the river. The back of the boat was beginning to drift from the bank, and Tony was leaning over trying to pull the rope up.

Two hours into a holiday that was probably not one of my better ideas, and I wished I could go home.

'Tony! Come here, now! Leave the rope.'

Fortunately he didn't argue. I gave it a burst in reverse again, swung the wheel over and snapped at him, 'Hold that!' I ran to the back, hauled the sodden rope out of the water and managed to jump ashore from about halfway along the boat, still with the end of the rope in my hand.

'Turn the engine off!' I called to him.

We hadn't been through that instruction either. Instead of turning the key, he pushed the throttle and the boat started to move forward again. I had a brief, awful vision of him disappearing up river alone, with both Sarah and I standing watching from the land.

'Tie that!' I barked, thrusting the rope at Sarah, and I leapt across the ever-widening gap, back onto the boat – just!

Tony had realized his mistake, and pulled the throttle backwards, so we were now in danger of reversing back downstream.

I hoped to God that Sarah had been a girl guide and knew something about knots, because that was another thing we'd neglected to cover before starting out. I flipped the throttle into neutral, and after a couple of seconds we came to a rather juddering stop as the rope pulled tight – and held.

I turned the engine off. Tony seemed to be holding his breath, watching me, probably waiting for an explosion of bad temper. But we were moored; both ends were tied up and no one had fallen in. I looked sideways at him. I think he realized I wasn't going to bite his head off, and a big grin spread across his face.

'Sorry, *Mum*!'

Chapter 26

I woke up stiff-necked, with a backache. I'd forgotten quite how uncomfortable boats could be. Perhaps if I'd kept the booking of the flashy model, the bedding might have been more luxurious. This boat was smaller than the original, but it was still designed to sleep more than four, which meant we had a cabin each, after a fashion. I had pinched what would have been the double bed in the centre of the boat, which meant I was by the tiny cooker, useful for late night coffee or early morning tea. What wasn't useful was that I had to completely dismantle my bed in order for us to have somewhere to sit and eat.

I put on the kettle, as quietly as I could. Despite all my reservations, I had actually quite enjoyed our first day. The initial mooring had not turned into a tragedy, and I hoped it was a manoeuvre that would improve. Nevertheless, I was happy to have a few moments alone. Those moments didn't last. Tony appeared first, in his pyjamas, shortly followed by Sarah, who had somehow managed to don sweatshirt and jeans. Despite it being summer, it was barely after half past six and there was still a nip in the air. That was just as well, because it had made me wrap myself in a blanket before they appeared, covering nothing more than a thin T-shirt and a pair of knickers underneath.

Tea consumed, I announced that I was going to attempt to get the shower to work.

'Can I use the loo first?'

'And me, please.'

I'd been spoilt. I wasn't used to sharing a bathroom.

Apart from sleeping on wooden boards, I had also forgotten how well people living on boats needed to know each other – and get on! I succeeded in finding all my clothes, while still draped in a blanket, and I took the whole lot into what was imaginatively described as a bathroom. The shower soaked more of my clothes than me, but I still had to put them on, before I could come out again. I decided that an eleven-year-old boy could appear in public in pyjamas, so I sent them both out on deck while I changed again.

It was the easiest way for each of us to get dressed in anything close to comfort, so two people at a time went outside, leaving the other the space to move around. When the make-up of personnel on the deck got to its third permutation, it was Tony and me. I was beginning to lose the feelings of enjoyment of the day before, and was just wondering what we would do if it rained, when Tony broke uncompromisingly into my daydreaming.

'Can I call you Mum?'

A very unsettling feeling crept into my stomach, and Hilary's comments catapulted into my head. 'My name's Alison, or Ally.'

'Doesn't feel right.'

I chose not to look at him. Maybe he did find that uncomfortable, I thought, clutching at straws, and I actually couldn't remember him ever calling me anything. There was a generation gap, after all. He was eleven. It might not have been easy for him to use my first name. I doubt he would have called his dad's mates by their first names. However, the amusement it had brought yesterday when we were messing around vanished abruptly.

I said very slowly, 'I am not your Mum.'

'I know.' He shrugged. 'But I'd like to call you that.'

The unsettled feeling was beginning to lean towards distinct foreboding. I had brought this on myself. Now I had to deal with it. 'If you just want to use it as your name for me, then okay, but I am not what your mum was to you, or should have been, and I am not going to be, Tony.'

I think I might just as well have said it to the fish. The first time he said it after that, Sarah stopped dead and stared at him in astonishment.

'It's just my name for her.' Obviously he'd heard part of what I'd said.

'Is it?' Sarah replied.

'Yes!' I said emphatically, hopefully, to both of them.

Perhaps he could just use it as a name, but by late morning, considering he'd never before needed to call me anything, his use of it every other sentence was becoming a little excessive. At least twice I didn't even register that anyone was talking to me. I wasn't used to responding to that particular title. Would I get used to it? Did I want to?

It was Sarah who snapped first.

'Mum?' he called.

'For God's sake, Tony, why don't you call her Dad instead? He only died two weeks ago. Is it that easy to replace him with someone else?'

She might as well have slapped him. He looked totally stunned. Sarah burst into tears and rushed to the back of the boat; Tony hurled himself at me, for reassurance, just as we were approaching our first lock!

It was a manned lock, thank God, but the keeper was waving us in as the gates were open, and I had lost all assistance. I pushed Tony away. 'We'll talk in a minute, go and find your sister.'

'No.'

'Oh shit!'

It wasn't my finest piece of boatmanship, but, under the circumstances, it was miraculous. I managed to slow us down before we cannoned into the gates at the far end, but we bumped – mercifully fairly gently – into the boat on our right. I raced out on deck, and the female half of the middle-aged owners of what I'd just hit gave me a reassuring smile.

'Toss the ropes over here, dear. I remember, it's hard when you're doing this alone.'

'I'm not alone,' I replied, probably looking as harassed as I felt. 'There's two kids in there having a strop!'

Her husband joined us, chuckling at my comment. 'Throw them in the river,' he said with a grin.

'Oh, don't remind me,' his wife said. 'He did that once to our son.'

'Did it help?'

219

She laughed. 'Yes, it did, actually. Except that he then had to jump in and pull him out. But I don't think we ever had such a well-behaved child as we did for the rest of that week.'

'Don't tempt me!' I said, and we all laughed.

The lock was getting close to full.

The man turned to go back inside. 'I'll edge forward and we'll move out first. Don't worry about the bumps, it'll do no damage. You just poodle off, pull in and chuck 'em overboard.'

'Thank you.'

'Good luck, dear.'

I did poodle off and I did pull in, and although the rest of the suggestion was tempting, I resisted. I shouted, as authoritatively as I could manage, 'Sarah, get the front rope, please, we're stopping.'

Anger, at myself as well as them, served this time to grant me the best piece of manoeuvring I'd ever done. Sarah secured the front rope and I stepped off the back, over a paper-thin gap, and secured the other. I looked up and there was a pub! The tables were set out almost all the way down to the river, and there was hardly anyone sitting there. I had no idea if one could be charged for being drunk in charge of a boat, but, right now, I didn't care.

'Fetch Tony, lock up and find a table. I'll get some drinks and then we'll talk.'

I knew a guy, when I was at college, who used to go to get a round of drinks in and order himself a large Scotch first. He would then swallow it down in one gulp and order himself another one, at the end of the round, to take out with the rest. I didn't gulp it down, but I did order a Scotch, as well as the orange juices and the lager. The barman had no idea how many of us there were.

I took a pretty large mouthful before I spoke. 'This is an incredibly hard time for all of us. I miss Derek, and you miss your dad, and yes, it was only two weeks ago that he died. Sarah, I don't believe that Tony's using me to replace him, and I couldn't do that anyway. I wouldn't even try. Nor am I trying to replace your mum. If Derek and I had got married, I still couldn't have replaced your mum.' I paused, thinking, Please don't ask me if that might have happened.

'Might that have happened?' Sarah asked.

'We'll never know.' That, certainly, was true. 'We all need mums and dads. Some people are lucky enough to have loving parents who live to be a hundred. Some people, like me, lose them before they should, and some people, like you two, lose them at the hardest times of their lives.'

I finished the Scotch.

'It's not fair. It really, really, really isn't fair. You did nothing wrong; don't ever think that life played this bloody awful trick on you because you did something wrong. None of this is your fault. You didn't deserve this to happen. But life isn't always fair, and it often kicks us in the guts right at the moment that we can least cope with it. And yet, somehow, it leaves us with just enough to be able to carry on. Sarah, you'll go back to school in September and start studying for your exams. That will feel like an added burden on top of everything else, but it's your future, and that study will take over, because it has to. Then you'll even start to feel excited about that future, and then probably feel guilty, because how can you get excited when your dad died just a few months ago? If you don't get excited your dad will never forgive you. He worked all his life so you *could* have a future. And Tony, he did the same for you. You have one more year and then you have to change schools. You and your mates will spend a good part of that year deciding where you want to go. You'll know what's right, because if it's right for you, it would have been right for your dad. He trusted both of you to know your own minds.' I drained the lager and stood up. 'I'm going for another drink. Don't go away. I haven't finished.'

I ordered another Scotch, as well as my lager. I think I could have drunk a bottle and walked a straight line without a quiver. I had never delivered a monologue like it in my life and, no, I hadn't finished. What I'd done so far was the easy bit.

I sat down again and stared from one wide-eyed expression to another. Up to that moment, the adrenalin had been pumping, but suddenly I felt so tired.

'Tony, you need a mum. Sarah, you probably did need a mum in the same way, but now you need that special friendship that your relationship with your mum might have become. What you both need is that complete trust in someone who cares for you. The kind of trust you know when you're a baby, that lasts if you're lucky. The kind of love you need is unique, and maybe none of us – none of us – will find it again until we meet someone so special that we want to marry them.'

The alcohol had taken hold, and I think I was now talking over their heads, but I had to finish – for me.

'I cannot be a substitute for your mother or your father. I can't give you that kind of love; I can't feel it. All I can do is give you my friendship. Right now that won't be enough for you, because friendship comes with restrictions. Selfish as it might sound, you don't come first, I do! But when it doesn't interfere with my own life, I'll do anything I can for you.'

I rubbed my hands over my face. They must have completely lost track of what I was talking about. I wasn't even sure if I was talking to them or to me. I had a friend named Mary, who was a teacher. When the kids in her class asked, 'What does the "M" stand for Miss?' she would reply, 'Yes, that's right!' If her first name could be 'Miss', I imagined I could live with mine being 'Mum', for a bit, anyway.

'Tony, if you want to call me Mum – as a name – I guess I can live with that. But do us all a favour and don't wear it out!'

I handed the boat keys to Sarah. 'Get back on board, both of you, and don't even think about untying anything! I'm just going for a walk.'

I wandered up the path, thinking about mums and dads who were no longer with us. There were some wild flowers growing on the bank and I paused and pulled one from the ground. I thought about plastic roses, then I tossed the flower into the water and watched it drift slowly away.

Chapter 27

Our next lock was less of a trauma, and once again we were lucky enough to steer straight in without mooring first. I did thump the rear of the boat on departure, and something inside fell on the floor with a crash, but I could see it wasn't a person, so I wasn't bothered.

'Can I drive?' This time he didn't add 'Mum' to the question.

'Okay, but no faster than we're going now.'

I went and sat on the bow; precisely what I'd told him he couldn't do. After a few moments Sarah came and joined me, but we didn't talk. I think just sitting together was enough to say that our last conversation had left no irresolvable ill feeling. It occurred to me that the two of us, where we were, would restrict Tony's view, but the river was straight for the next stretch, and he seemed to be going straight. Having decided I could dash inside if he began to veer off in any odd direction, I just sat there, lost in my own thoughts. Sarah grabbing my arm brought me rapidly out of my reverie. A boat was heading towards us, apparently driven by a complete lunatic. The speed he was doing would have towed water skiers, and he was throwing up the most immense bow wave.

'Quick!' I shouted, but we couldn't move that quickly.

The wave hurled itself right over the front of the boat, completely soaking the pair of us, and rained down, with a great slap onto the windscreen. It must have startled Tony so much that he probably left his seat. Sarah and I, at least, knew we were going to get wet; Tony couldn't have had any idea what was coming – we'd blocked his sight. Whether he'd just let go of everything in shock, I don't know, but the remains of the wave threw our boat sideways, rocking it violently, and suddenly we were heading straight for the bank. I was torn between scrabbling through the water to get inside to steer, and making sure Sarah didn't slip.

'Just grab hold of something!' I yelled at her, and slithered into the cabin. I pushed Tony out of the way and swung the wheel, while frantically slamming the throttle into reverse. Boats don't respond instantly. We ploughed into the bank. Sarah had braced herself, although it must have given her arms quite a wrench. Tony fell on the floor. We bounced back out towards the middle of the river and finally came to an unstable halt right across the main stream.

'Are you all right?' I shouted.

Sarah gave me a slightly shaky wave. Tony clambered to his feet.

'Wow! Cool!'

We pulled in to the first available mooring. It wasn't one of our better efforts, and one of the ropes came loose, but we rescued the situation without further mishap. Two of us were saturated. I told Sarah to get herself into some dry clothes and took Tony out on deck; I hoped she'd be quick, because I was starting to shiver, and the sky was looking threatening. I was certain that Tony wouldn't care if the rain arrived and soaked him. He was still on a high and would probably live off tales of the incident for the whole of the next school term.

Finally, it was my turn to change, and just as I'd pulled on a dry top, I heard a noise. I'd placed my mobile phone in the cutlery drawer for safety. Just as well it wasn't in my pocket half an hour ago, I thought, as I retrieved it from vibrating the knives and forks quite tunefully. 'Hello?'

'Ally, it's Mark.'

This wasn't going to be a social call to inquire about the holiday.

'What's happened?'

'Mickey buggered up a connection.'

My heart sank. Mickey was a plumber; usually very good, but occasionally careless.

'Go on, tell me.'

'It must have been leaking all night and just filling up in the eaves space, but we didn't see it, till it came through the light and blew everything.'

'Oh God. How much damage?'

'Well, part of the ceiling's come down and the decs on one wall have had it. The carpet's a bit of a mess.'

I didn't answer straightaway – I couldn't – and he went on. 'Clients aren't too happy.'

Eventually I managed to speak. 'I bet they're not. Anything else?' As if that wasn't enough.

'The settee and one armchair, but they may dry out. It also injured the cat.'

At that moment I felt as if it was my world that had fallen in, not a client's lounge. I was only a few miles away, but I might as well have been at the other end of the earth. This had never happened to me before. Since I'd taken over the business we'd had a few inevitable mishaps, a few minor leaks, but nothing like this. And I couldn't get there!

'I've checked all Mickey's work, now. It's not leaking anymore.'

'I should bloody well hope it isn't!' My head was swimming. I didn't know what to do. My car was over a day's journey away, by boat. I couldn't leave the kids and leap into a taxi. I couldn't tell Mark to come and fetch me; he was needed there. I could abandon the boat and our belongings and drag the kids off in the taxi with me, but would that achieve anything? If I was to be of any help, I needed my tools and my car. Now I didn't know if I was making excuses. I was only too aware that I didn't even want to see what had happened. I may not have been there, but I was still in charge. I realized Mark was speaking.

'Les is here now, we're starting to clear up.'

'I can't get there straightaway.'

'I know you can't. They do know you're on holiday, they're not blaming you.'

Aren't they? I thought to myself. 'I'll get back as soon as I can, but it won't be today, I've got to get back to the boatyard and that's through two locks, and this thing doesn't go very fast, and then I've got to get home and drop the kids.' I was gabbling now. I wanted Mark to say that I didn't have to go back, but I knew he wouldn't. He needed me there. I felt sick. 'Tell them I'll be there as soon as I can. Stress that they will be compensated for everything, and just don't stop apologizing.'

He still could have said, Don't come back. 'Okay, I'll tell them.'

'I'll phone you when I have some idea of how long I'll be.'

And he still could have said it. 'Sorry!'

I buried my head in my hands. I'd wanted to be the boss, now I had to take the responsibility that went with it. My current responsibilities had come inside and were watching me. What did I say about life not being fair? I asked myself. I looked at both kids. 'I've got to go home.'

Tony looked as if he was about to cry, but it was Sarah's response that astounded me.

'Did you know this was going to happen?'

'I beg your pardon?'

'All the talk about the fact that sometimes holidays go wrong and we might have to go home.'

'Just a minute...' But she didn't let me finish.

'Or is this just that selfish part of friendship?'

I wasn't certain how I kept silent. Inside I was raging.

'Well, you've done it before, haven't you? Said something to fob people off, when you really meant something else!'

I very slowly got up, went out on deck and jumped onto the bank. I could not have let myself answer her. I heard someone else on the deck, but I didn't look round, I just wandered up the path. It wasn't long before a bewildered eleven-year-old called to me.

'Do we really have to go home?'

I took a deep breath and turned back to the boat. I stretched out a hand and he jumped ashore.

'Mark and a couple of other guys are working in a bungalow for me. One of them made a mistake and caused a flood. The flood has ruined an entire room, including carpet and furniture, and the ceiling fell down on their cat.'

He giggled at that. 'Is the cat dead?'

'I hope not. But Mark and the others work for me, and that makes it my fault.'

'But it's not. You weren't there.'

I nearly said to him that I should have been, or even that a big part of me, right now, wished I had been – instead of here. Would that have made a difference? It would as far as the latest conflict with Sarah was concerned. In relation to the work disaster, I wasn't sure. Would I have checked all Mickey's work before leaving last night? Actually, I probably would have done, and that made me feel a hundred times worse.

'The responsibility to put it right is up to me. I have to talk to the people and make sure that everything is repaired and redecorated and all new stuff bought to replace what's damaged. I have to go home.'

I think he understood. I knew he was desperately disappointed, but it made sense to him. 'Will you have to get them a new cat?'

I smiled. 'I'll probably have to pay the vet's bills.'

Maybe he didn't understand, totally. 'Why do you have to pay for it, if you didn't do it?'

'I pay for insurance for me and my guys, and for what we do, in case things go wrong, but it will cost me quite a bit as well, I imagine. I'm in charge. Ultimately it's up to me.'

I had forked out premiums for some huge amount of public liability insurance, year after year, and so far – fortunately – I had never had to use it. I wasn't even certain I knew how it worked. I doubt that fate could have picked a worse time to let me find out.

I realized that we'd ambled a long way up the towpath, so I turned round and we walked back. The last thing I needed was Sarah to go off in a huff in the other direction. I had no desire to talk to her, but she was yet another of the responsibilities currently weighing me down.

Chapter 28

The atmosphere had lasted all evening. We had found a place to eat and the conversation had consisted of little more than what each of us wanted from the menu. I had made them pack up most of their belongings before we went to bed.

We had cleared the first lock, after one unscheduled full circle outside the gates, watched by far too many other boats, and now we were heading towards the second. Progress was agonizingly slow. I didn't want to see the chaos my workforce had created, but I did need to get to it as soon as possible. Now, this gently paced, tranquil holiday transport had become a sluggish, exasperating impediment to achieving that end. The sun was out and I'd let both kids sit out on the bow, glad to have them nowhere near me. The mood I was in, I wasn't sure I'd stop if one of them fell in. As the lock came into view, Sarah entered the cabin.

'I'm sorry,' she said.

'Okay, thank you.'

She left again to get to her post at the front rope. It didn't put everything right, but it helped a bit. I was still mad with her, but I was also mad with me. Perhaps it was harder to put that right.

We had to wait ages for the lock; it was full of boats coming towards us. I tried to calm down by telling myself how much worse it would have been if we'd gone any further – the next locks we would have encountered were unmanned. Eventually it was our turn, but when it came to exit, one boat in front got it totally wrong and finished up sideways, blocking everybody. Just as I was contemplating murder, Tony stuck his head in the door. 'We were never *that* bad!' He seemed to have recovered from his disappointment. He had, after all, had a bit of a holiday.

The boatyard owner was very surprised to see us. When I told him something had happened and we had to go home, he looked genuinely concerned. He had been aware of the disaster that had struck before we took the boat out. I waited for him to check everything and make sure that we'd left it all as it should be, but he waved an arm dismissively and helped us to the car with our belongings.

'I'll give you a note,' he said. 'You can take it to the holiday firm and they can sort out a refund.'

This holiday had been all refunds so far, and none of the causes were good ones.

I had spoken to Mark again early that morning and given him some idea of when I might get back, but I wasn't going to achieve that time. I had also left a message at home to tell one brother or the other what was going on, but neither had contacted me. I hoped someone was in, because otherwise I'd just have to dump the kids and leave them there alone. I got hold of Mark while driving home and revised my ETA.

'How's things?'

'Still drying out.'

I didn't think I wanted to know any more.

'Okay, I'll see you shortly.'

We pulled into the drive. No one was home.

Shit,' I muttered. It had become a much-used word in the last few hours. I opened the door and looked hopefully for a note to say if anyone was coming back at any particular time. My brothers weren't that considerate.

'Sorry, but I'm just going to have to dump everything and shoot off. Can you get the wet stuff out of the bags and chuck it in the utility room. Find yourselves something to eat and I'll see you later. I don't know how long I'll be, I'm afraid.'

I drove out. I was hardly looking my best for grovelling apologies to irate clients, but at least I was showing willing and turning up as soon as I could.

*

Mark had been the master of understatement. The room was in ruins, but he had obviously managed to make enough apologies and offers of compensation for the owners to be relatively calm. I think it helped that the cat had only had three stitches.

I had not bothered to take any tools or work clothes; by the time I'd left my house it was almost four o'clock, so not a huge amount more was going to get done that day. All I had taken was a harassed me, full of expressions of regret.

Les was a reassuring figure amid the chaos. 'Good holiday?' he asked with a smirk.

I looked up at the missing section of ceiling. 'I think this is worse.'

'Sure?'

'I'm not sure which will take longer to fix.'

'At least we can repair this,' he said. 'It only costs money.'

I went across and looked at the settee. It now had a grey-tinged floral pattern, with a very large water mark. The space heater that was trying to draw gallons of water out of the carpet wasn't going to solve that one. It was only one settee and one chair that were damaged, but they matched an even bigger settee and another chair. Mark's assessment that only the decorations on one wall were ruined was technically accurate, but the entire room would have to be done, and it was a large room, with very expensive wallpaper. The ceiling light now consisted of a batten holder and a bare bulb. I remembered it had been a multiple wooden arrangement, now presumably ruined, as well. Unfortunately, it had matched the wall lights, and I doubted anyone still manufactured them. I looked down. Maybe the carpet would dry out, and maybe it would clean up, but it looked to me as if it had shrunk. I hoped that was my imagination.

'Can you take off that skirting board; I expect it's sodden behind there.'

I left them making more mess and went back to talk to the owners. 'I really am most terribly sorry,' I said to them again. 'Maybe we can sit down tomorrow and talk about new furniture and decorations and replacing everything that's been damaged.'

I desperately needed to check the exact terms of my insurance before I got too carried away.

'That would be good, thank you. We do know these things happen, but it was an awful shock.'

'I'm sure it was. Were you here?'

'Not when everything fell down, luckily. Mark met us at the door; we'd been out shopping.'

'Thank God you weren't in the room. How's Tiger?'

'He's getting lots of fuss, so I think he's all right. And how are you?'

'Oh,' I shrugged. 'It's not been the easiest of times.'

'This hasn't helped, has it?'

I attempted some sort of smile. I couldn't deal with their sympathy considering what we'd done to their home. We had only gone to put a coat of paint on their conservatory and run an extra radiator out to it.

'How are the children doing?'

Mark must have filled them in on the whole story.

'Obviously they're finding it hard.' I needed to get away. If they were any kinder, I would go to pieces. I needed to stay mad with the world, and with Mickey in particular. I excused myself, before they said anything else nice, and arranged a time for the morning to sit down and talk. I returned to what had once been a room.

'Les said see you tomorrow.'

Tomorrow was Saturday. We didn't work Saturdays, but no one was going to say they couldn't work this Saturday.

'Right, we might as well go too.'

I called out goodbye to the owners, and she popped her head out of the kitchen. 'You take care of yourself.'

We shut the front door and Mark asked, 'Are you okay?'

I looked up at him and my eyes filled up. 'No! I don't know what the insurance covers. I don't even know how I claim. I've never had to do this. I don't know if we need estimates for things or if they pay for new stuff, and if so up to what value, and I don't know who pays for the redecoration and...'

He grabbed hold of me, as the tears began to fall freely.

'Hey, hey, it's all right.'

'No, it's not. Nothing's all right.'

He held on to me a bit longer. 'Are you okay to drive?'

I nodded.

'Then get in the car, drive carefully home and I'll be right behind you. I'm not going to let you sort this out alone. We'll have a drink and look at it all together. It will be okay.'

I did what I was told and got in the car, but I didn't believe that it would be okay – any of it – maybe ever again.

*

Sarah certainly didn't expect to see Mark. Neither did she seem very pleased about it. Tony just said hello. His mood appeared to have sunk. I supposed that reality had set in for both of them. They were back here; there was no holiday on the horizon and there was still a huge loss to deal with. No brothers had turned up either, to give them someone to talk to.

Sarah did make an effort to be pleasant. She'd likely noticed how rough I looked. 'Were things very bad?'

'They're certainly not good,' Mark answered her. 'One blown plumbing fitting can cause an awful lot of mess.'

'Can I make you some tea?'

I appreciated her effort. It couldn't have been easy. She may well have spent all the time I was away thinking about what she was going to say to me, and now I'd ruined it by arriving with Mark in tow.

'Thanks, but I think we need something stronger. Would you like a glass of wine?'

'Oh, okay, yes please.'

'Can I have one, Mum?'

Mark leant back out of their eye line, his eyes widening in surprise, and mouthed at me, '*Mum*?'

I couldn't respond. The kids could see me.

Mark moved forward again and said to Tony, 'You can share my glass of beer, or have a taste of it, anyway.'

That produced a smile.

We sat in the lounge and I got drinks for everyone. I'm sure Tony had tried beer before. I don't suppose he'd liked it the first time, and his face told us his opinion hadn't changed. True to eleven-year-old form, he persisted trying for a few more mouthfuls before he gave up.

'One day you'll wish you still didn't like it.'

He looked as if he doubted that and ran off to find one of the bottles of lemonade we had brought back with us.

'I'd better find the insurance policy.'

'Ally, sit down. Have another drink. We can look at it later. Just unwind for a bit.'

'Aren't you seeing Melanie?'

'No, not tonight, but I am going to be hungry, so where's the takeaway menu?'

'I'll get it.' Sarah was being very helpful. Maybe she had decided what she was going to say to me, and maybe it would have been difficult, particularly if it involved any further apologies. I knew only too well that apologizing wasn't easy. Initially, Mark's appearance would have ruined her resolve, but now the fact that he was not departing at once might have saved her instead.

Mark had saved me too, in more ways than one.

Chapter 29

It was six o'clock on Saturday morning and the last thing in the world I wanted to happen – happened. Mark walked out of my bedroom and found himself face to face with Sarah. I heard her startled 'Oh!' from where I was, still in bed, and groaned. Mark's attempt to make things sound as if this was quite normal, even though he was probably as startled as her, made me groan even more.

'Good morning, how are you?'

She obviously didn't reply, so he added, 'Do you want the bathroom? I can wait.'

All I heard after that was her door closing.

He poked his head back round into my room. 'Oops!' he said, and went back to the bathroom.

The kids had gone to bed quite early, as we had started peering at insurance policies. Had they heard a male voice later, they would have assumed it was Phil or Andy, neither of whom had appeared at all.

I climbed, gloomily, out of bed and collected some clothes together. Whatever conversation might have been on the cards for today, between Sarah and me, the content had undoubtedly just changed. I didn't relish the prospect.

The sound of Tony running down the stairs was the next piece of bad news. Now we'd meet him in the kitchen as well. I wasn't daft enough to think that, at his age, he wouldn't know what was going on, but I didn't believe it would affect him in quite the same way. He might be disappointed, or even in one respect a little jealous, but in many ways he'd already got what he wanted from me. I was meeting his immediate needs, and I think he was beginning to feel more secure with me. It was, possibly, a fragile security, but it wasn't a major problem for *him* any more – only for me.

Sarah needed security and affection and was afraid to show she needed it, but my guess was that she had already started to feel that dependency on me and was now terrified of losing it again. Fear often makes us lash out and say harsh and hurtful things. Now she would have more reason to be afraid and even more reason to lash out. And all those problems, I thought, before I'd figured out exactly what it was that *I* needed!

Mark came back, gave me a doleful look and sat on the bed to put on his socks. 'Don't kids stay in bed till midday any more?'

'Not these two, sadly,' although I had thought that if we were away before seven, we should miss them. When it had become obvious that Mark was going to stay the night, I had suggested the early departure time to prevent any chance of this sort of confrontation.

'How's she going to react?' he asked.

'With luck, she'll sulk in her room until we've left.'

'You've still got to come back later.'

I raised my eyebrows at him. He chuckled.

I went off to the bathroom. Mark hadn't moved when I returned; he wasn't going to go down alone. By the time I'd finished getting dressed, I knew my luck had run out. I'd heard Sarah go along to the bathroom and then straight down the stairs.

Mark and I sloped down like a couple of naughty schoolchildren being sent to the headmaster. I believe that Sarah had made a decision not to say anything, which would have been very restrained, considering that she was probably feeling betrayed – or that her father had been. She just nodded to both of us, but as we moved further into the room Tony saw Mark.

'What are *you* doing here?'

'I'm going to make some tea,' he replied.

I thought that was as good an answer as any.

'Have you been here all night?'

I didn't want this conversation and, apparently, neither did Sarah.

She snapped at her brother, 'Oh, don't be an idiot!' Then, very suddenly, she burst into tears.

I moved towards her, but the tautly held emotions had snapped.

'Leave me alone,' she spluttered. 'How *could* you!'

'Sarah…'

'I really began to believe that Dad meant something to you.'

'Of course he did.'

'Did?' she shouted. 'Did? He doesn't mean much now, does he? Not even his memory is worth anything any more, is it?'

'Come on, that's not fair,' Mark said.

'Please stay out of it,' I said quietly to him.

'Yes.' Sarah turned on him. 'You stay out of it. You just walked in and took over before my father had been dead much more than two weeks!'

I think if I had been Mark, I might have slapped her. Instead he said, 'I could say that your dad walked in and took over after I'd known Ally for about five years.' He held up his hands in mock surrender. 'But I'll stay out of it.' With remarkable reserve he walked across the room and started making himself a cup of tea.

I think she was going to shout something else at him, but having opened her mouth, she stopped. In that instant, the fighting teenager became a frightened child. 'What are we going to do now?' she started to sob, and then, before I realized what was happening, she ran to the front door, threw it open and was gone.

I was stunned and didn't move for a few seconds, by which time Tony had rushed over and grabbed hold of me. I wanted to push him away, I wanted to hug him. I wanted to shout after Sarah that I was sorry. I wanted to slam the door after her. Most of all, I wanted to cry.

Mark looked at me. 'Oh, God,' he muttered.

I detached Tony and hurried to the front door. There was no sign of her. 'Sarah!' I shouted. I couldn't make myself shout, 'I'm sorry'.

'Sarah, come on, love, come back!'

It was a long front garden. How she had managed to disappear in that short time, I couldn't imagine. I looked round both sides of the house, but there was no trace. I jogged down the drive to the road. Nothing! She had to be hiding. She could probably even see me, and that thought made me angry. Right, I said to myself, you've made your protest, young lady, I've showed my immediate concern, now it's up to you. I walked back to the house, where Tony was hovering, anxiously, by the front door. My anger faded away; he looked so frightened. I took his hand. 'Come on, she'll be back in a minute.'

There was no purpose to be gained in debating who was at fault. Maybe both of us; maybe neither of us. We both had needs, and each was very obviously having a disastrous effect on the other. I doubted that she would be back in a minute. That would be too soon to climb down, and I briefly remembered a time when I had come very close to running away. Then I had told myself that if I did, I wasn't coming back at all.

I didn't know what to do. She might just reappear, but she might not. I could wait for a while; I *would* wait for a while. But maybe she hadn't been hiding and hadn't seen that I cared enough to go after her straightaway. I knew I couldn't just let her go off and do nothing. She might not go very far, but then again she might. This was not familiar territory to her and she could very easily head into some of the vast expanses of local woods and get totally lost. If she had just run to put some distance between us, she might already be lost, and the longer I left it, the worse it could get. I also needed to go to work. I'd promised the clients, whose bungalow had been decimated by my workmen, that I would be there this morning. I couldn't leave Tony here alone; he was tearful and he was frightened, and I couldn't let him lose his sister.

Mark put a mug of tea on the table for me. 'Sorry, I guess I made things worse.'

'No, only I can do that.'

'Go and find her,' he said. 'I'll take the insurance stuff and sort it out. I can make all the calls and find out what we need to know. Okay, that makes me a coward as far as Sarah's concerned, but I doubt she would want it to be me that rescued her, even if she'd fallen down a mineshaft.'

'There aren't any mineshafts, are there?' A moment of panic shot through me.

He gave me a compassionate smile and shook his head. 'Let me deal with the mess at the bungalow. I'll tell them you've had a family crisis. They'll understand. They'll be fine as long as things are repaired and they get a shiny new lounge with all its fixtures and fittings. Anyway, it should be me that puts it right; I was in charge when Mickey cocked it up.'

I let go of Tony's hand, my eyes a watery blur, and wrapped my arms round Mark's neck.

'You're an angel. Thank you for being here for me.'

Tony was looking fretful, as if he needed to keep the physical contact.

Mark ruffled his hair. 'You stick to this "Mum" of yours, kid, everything will be all right, I promise you.' Then he walked off to the lounge and returned carrying the insurance documents.

I was still in a daze. He bent slightly and gave me a very gentle kiss on the forehead.

'I will always be here for you. Whether or not we go our separate routes, I will *always* be here for you. That's what best friends do.'

Before I could even begin to take in what he'd said, he had squatted down in front of Tony. 'And as a friend to you, young man, I'm going to make you a promise. I'll take you for your first pint, when you're old enough, and see if you still prefer lemonade.'

Tony stared wide-eyed at him, then, slowly, one of the most heart-warming smiles I have ever seen spread across his face.

And then my new best friend kissed me on the cheek and left the house.

Chapter 30

I had this crazy hope that Sarah might be sitting outside when I reopened the door, but it wasn't to be. I walked to the end of the drive again, with Tony constantly within touching distance. No sign of a distraught teenager. What would a normally sensible person do if they decided to throw a tantrum and run off, particularly if they had absolutely no knowledge of the surrounding area? I was very aware that the answers to my questions would depend entirely on whether she ever intended to come back. If she didn't, I might never find her, but if she did, surely she would need to stay close to what was familiar?

One third of the offspring that had once told our dad he hadn't bought enough land, briefly cursed him for buying any of it. What we called the garden was about half an acre behind the house. That part was fairly open, as was the frontage, which spread sideways to rather vague boundaries buried among trees and shrubs. There was a huge garage that my father had erected, which had never housed a car in its life, but that was locked. Sarah couldn't get in there. If she had decided to stay on our property somewhere near the house, she would eventually reach barbed-wire fencing, which should have made the limits obvious, so the most she could do was hide behind the garage or in the equally large garden shed. Those parts were easy to check, but added to that was about another four acres. There were two fields, where we all swore that one day we'd have horses, or maybe a cow or sheep or something very self-sufficient. There were a couple of old dilapidated barns at the ends of the fields, and behind those the shrubs and trees became thicker and thicker. Just beyond the wooded area was our boundary. It wasn't a series of mineshafts, but it was a rather nasty ditch. The woodland opened up quite suddenly, and went downhill equally suddenly, towards a slippery bank, rocks and semi-stagnant water. Both my brothers and I had fallen in it, in the past.

I walked back up towards the house, Tony attached to one hand, wondering where to start looking. A car drove in behind us, and I swung round. I would have preferred it to be Phil, but any brother would be a help right now. Andy gave us a wave, pulled up and got out of his car.

'Hi, I gather you had a rather curtailed trip.'

'Yes, just a bit, but it's got worse since then. Where's Phil?'

'Haven't a clue. What's happened?'

I let out a deep sigh, not quite knowing where to start. 'Sarah's run off.'

He stared at me. 'What caused that?'

I looked down at the ground and unconsciously put an arm around Tony. 'Basically, because Mark stayed last night. It didn't go down very well.'

He gave me shrug, as if to say, So what? 'Well, you need a life too.'

Yes, that would be your view, I thought, but I said, 'Unfortunately, we haven't yet got to that sort of conversation.'

He followed us inside and headed to the kitchen and put on the kettle.

'I need a coffee, and then I'm all yours. Where have you looked so far?'

I smiled at him, with gratitude. Perhaps he was as good as Phil.

'I haven't, it didn't happen that long ago. I've just been trying to convince myself that she couldn't have gone far, because she doesn't know anywhere around here.'

'You're probably right,' he said. 'Do you want tea?'

'Yes, please. Tony?'

A dejected head shook a negative response.

My brother continued making the drinks. 'Okay, where would you like me to look?'

I was beginning to feel drained. This could turn out to be an unending search, and if we did find her, I had no idea what was going to happen. I just knew that I had to find her. Andy pushed a mug of tea towards me. It was the second time that morning that someone had made me tea while I was in a daze. We drank in silence.

'Right,' Andy said, 'You check the shed and the barns; I'll head straight for the ditch.'

We both had the same fear.

'And you, young man, where are you going to look?'

'He's staying with me,' I said firmly.

The shed was empty. It was a long walk across the field to the barns, and I did it screwing my head round in all directions as I went. That slowed me down, as did having a youngster attached to my left hand. The grass over the field desperately needed cutting, and it slowed our progress even more.

'Shouldn't we shout out her name?' Tony asked.

'No. I don't think she'll want to be found, just yet.'

'Why not?'

'She's hurt and she's angry, and she needs time to think.'

'Because you had sex with Mark?'

That wasn't quite what I expected him to say!

'I think she feels', I went on carefully, 'that I don't care about you two as much any more.'

'Why?'

'Oh, Tony.' I turned round to face him and breathed in deeply. 'When you think about me, who do you think I am?'

He started to reply instantly, and then he paused and frowned in thought. 'I'd like to think you were my new mum.'

The breath I'd taken in, I exhaled very, very slowly. 'Sarah may very well want to think the same, but she hasn't been able to say that, and now she thinks it isn't possible.'

'Why isn't it?'

'To her, that could only happen while your dad was my boyfriend. You both would still have a dad, and maybe, in time, I could have become your new mum.'

'So why can't it still happen?'

'It can,' I replied.

Tony responded with something, but I didn't hear a word. I suddenly realized precisely what I'd just said. Had I answered him because that was what he wanted to hear? Do comments like that leap out of the subconscious, when one's not keeping a tight rein on them? I had never wanted children. I couldn't even make myself consider if it was possible that my attitude had changed. I just felt very confused.

'Mum?'

I blinked my focus back to the present, and for a few seconds the very conscious part of me wanted to pull my hand away from the one tugging at it.

'If you became my new mum…'

Now I did pull my hand away and held it up to silence him. 'Let's just find Sarah and make sure she's okay. Then we'll talk about this.'

He gave a philosophical shrug and moved off to continue towards the barns.

The first was empty. I had my hand on the door of the second when my mobile phone rang. Tony jumped, I jumped and I grabbed the phone from my pocket. I didn't even pause to see who was calling.

'Hello?'

'Ally, Andy. I've been all along the ditch – nothing.'

'Thank God for that. Hold on, I'm just at the second barn.'

I gave him a running commentary as I opened the door and went inside, but it was empty.

'Right. I'll come back through the woods a different way and see you at the house.'

'Okay. Thank you.'

We turned round and walked back across the field. I found myself reflecting on our conversation. It had had two very different effects. Tony didn't seem to need to hold my hand any more and I definitely needed to phone Hilary.

At one stage I caught sight of a movement in some bushes and began to jog towards it, but before I'd got very far, a large cock pheasant shot out with a raucous squawk. Tony aimed a pretend shotgun at it and said, 'Pow!'

Yes, he was distinctly more secure. As for me, I think at that moment I felt more insecure than ever. About everything.

We reached the house. There was still no sign of Sarah, but Phil had turned up. I was extremely relieved about that. *I* needed a substitute dad, whatever two kids might want or need. I related what had happened and left both brothers planning out a search strategy while I went to the phone.

'Hilary, it's me.'

She arrived shortly after Phil and Andy had both driven off in different directions to comb the local streets. Phil had decided I ought to stay at the house, just in case Sarah came back. I was beginning to have a horrible gnawing feeling that that was becoming less and less likely, but it did make sense for someone to be there. It just made me feel utterly useless, not actually *doing* anything. So far, Derek's two kids had disrupted quite a few lives.

'Have you phoned the police?'

I had hoped her first question might have been, How are you? I needed some care and affection too.

'Not yet, I hope we'll find her before we have to do that.'

It was her second question. 'And how are you doing?'

I felt tears threatening. 'I honestly don't know. All I do know is that we need to find her, before I can think straight about anything.'

'And when she turns up, you'll probably blow your top at her.'

'You're right, I probably will.'

'Just like a real mother!'

Sometimes Hilary could read me too well. There was no necessity to repeat the conversation I'd had with Tony. I'm sure she could see it all in my face. But, just like a real mum, as the time went on and there was no sign of Sarah, my desire to strangle her for worrying us all turned to deeper concern.

The boys came back. They had both run out of ideas of where to look. Phil had inquired at the train station, but if she had been there, no one remembered seeing a lone teenager. That hadn't been a real possibility, although it was good of him to think of it. Hilary and I had checked her room. This was not a pre-planned running away episode. She had no bag with her, therefore no money and, worst of all, no mobile phone. She had to be on foot, or – God forbid – thumbing a lift.

I was stubbornly fighting against a three-to-one majority in favour of calling the police, when a ghastly thought burrowed its way into my dazed brain.

'We can't!' I suddenly announced, with such force that they all turned to stare at me. I looked from one to the other, my face probably a picture of white shock. 'I never did phone social services!'

Andy let out a sigh that said, So what? Phil and Hilary continued to stare. I think they both, at that moment, started to see the various implications of my – probably unforgivable – oversight.

'You could say that lots of things have happened over the last few days,' Phil remarked. He was giving me a let-out, but his tone did not sound altogether approving.

'And what do I tell them, when I do get round to phoning? That I think I'm a completely responsible adult?' I looked with desperation at Hilary. 'One that's quite capable of being a parent to two children, who became orphans over a fortnight ago, but – oh, sorry – I just happen to have neglected to mention that to anyone! What the hell are they going to think? Sorry I didn't phone you, but the kids seemed okay, I was looking after them, I was caring for them, it's just that now I seemed to have misplaced one of them?'

Hilary got up. I think she was going to give me a hug, but I bolted out of my chair away from her.

'I didn't phone because I didn't want to have to answer what it was that *I* wanted!' I ran my hands through my hair in exasperation. 'I didn't consider them! Only me! I couldn't make that phone call because I couldn't face making that decision. And now Sarah could be anywhere – or dead!'

Tony let out a huge sob.

'She's not dead, Tony,' Hilary said in a remarkably calm voice. 'Ally's just worried about her, that's all. We *will* find her.'

I was pacing around the room like a caged lion, and I'm surprised no one slapped me to calm me down.

'We can go out and drive around again,' Phil said. 'She could have gone into any one of a dozen shops. She might just have been inside somewhere as we went past. You say she's got no money with her, but she can look. She may even have found the library.'

'Maybe she needs another maths book?' Tony suggested timidly.

I swung round and looked at him, remembering Sarah's excuse for going to the chemist. 'Oh.' I stopped pacing and closed my eyes for a second. I didn't care what two brothers and a best friend thought of my outbursts, but Tony? I forced myself to smile at him. 'Maybe you're right.'

He was still looking frightened, but there was a genuine hope in his eyes that he might have had a good idea.

Andy appeared at my right shoulder. He put a glass in my hand. 'Whoever goes out to drive around, it's not going to be you, so get that down you.'

'I'll make some tea,' Hilary said, sensibly. 'Let's just run through some ideas of where to look. If we come up with nothing, and we think that she could be lost in the woods, then we may have to call the police, but we'll do our best to find her before we get to that stage.'

This time I readily accepted a hug.

I couldn't think of anywhere that she might have gone deliberately. There were no places around here that she had visited with her dad that might hold special memories. We hadn't even collected his ashes yet, or talked about where to scatter them. There was no memorial anywhere to Derek. The last place she knew he had been was the hospital, but she hadn't seen him there. She didn't even know where it was. The last reminder she would have seen of him was his car.

His car!

I had been, of all places, in the loo, when the thought struck me, and I rushed back to the crowd of gloomy faces in the kitchen, still hanging on to an unfastened pair of jeans.

'Do you think she could have remembered how to get to the car yard?'

'What car yard?'

'Where they took Derek's car.'

'But we drove there.'

'So? It's not that far away.'

'And you think she could remember it on foot?'

'Well, it wasn't a complicated route.'

Phil stared at me for a second or two, then got up. 'Come on.'

Hilary said, 'I'll stay here with Tony.'

I spotted the car as we turned the corner. It was on top of about three other wrecks, a heavy chain forcing a huge dent into its roof, awaiting transportation to somewhere else to be turned into a completely flattened lump of metal that would mean nothing to anyone, except me, and a lonely-looking girl staring at it through a chain-link fence.

I simply walked over and stood beside her. She glanced round to see who it was, with no surprise and, fortunately, no instant reaction of running away from me. I put an arm gently round her waist.

'Let's go home.'

Chapter 31

I didn't blow my top and Sarah didn't apologize for worrying us. Phil said nothing as we got back in the car. He simply drove home as if we'd been collecting her from some pre-arranged pickup point. Andy had probably seen us arrive, before we reached the front door, and by the time we got inside he'd disappeared. Hilary seemed to gauge the mood and said nothing either. Only Tony, tearfully, ran up to his sister as if she had just returned from the dead.

Phil drifted off to do his own thing. Hilary said that she needed to go shopping. She offered to get some bits and pieces for me and took Tony with her. Having seen that his sister was alive and breathing and obviously unhurt, he was quite happy to go. I made Sarah some coffee and myself a cup of tea. I would have preferred something considerably stronger, but I felt I needed a clear head. I suggested we sat in the garden, and she followed me outside. It was all very controlled. Part of me wanted to slap her face, and I was absolutely certain that part of her wanted to do the same to me. This was not going to be an easy conversation, and I doubted that 'sorry' would be part of anyone's dialogue.

'Mark and I have known each other a long time.'

'I know. You've said that before.' She was calm, but still seemed resentful.

'And, yes, I do sleep with him occasionally.'

'Did you while my dad was around?'

258

She still wanted an argument, and I had to make sure she didn't get one.

'No.' I couldn't spontaneously recall if that was totally accurate, but I refused to search my conscience. I also had to make sure that I wasn't advocating casual sex to a fifteen-year-old, so this wasn't going to be a comfortable discussion from any viewpoint.

'So, you just picked up again with Mark as soon as Dad wasn't around?'

I felt as if I was being goaded into an argument. 'No,' I answered quite calmly. 'It just happened. You know why we had to come back from the boat. As far as my job's concerned, it was the worst day I've ever had in my life. Mark and I were both a bit shocked, and feeling sorry for ourselves and each other.'

I recalled my conversation with Hilary, about needing comforting.

'So even if Dad was around, it might still have happened?'

God, I thought, she really does want a row. 'I hardly think so!' I had to make it sound as if that was a totally unacceptable suggestion on her part, and I wasn't going to trawl through my own integrity. It didn't bear that close scrutiny. 'Mark and I are not an item,' I went on.

She looked up at me. 'But you were!'

I think I'd just trapped myself into the casual sex admission. 'No, not as such.' I escaped her disapproval on that count, because she'd suddenly found something else that could start an altercation.

'He said that Dad had broken up your relationship!'

'No, he didn't. All he said was that he had known me for years before your dad appeared. He was just trying to make a point.'

'But you're likely to become an item now, aren't you?'

I wasn't sure I could answer that one. Mark had said something about 'if we went our separate routes', and then described himself as my best friend. Maybe he had picked that very moment to make his comment, a moment when I was too confused about everything else to take it in. He could have been trying to tell me something that he didn't have the courage to say at another time. I had never really considered if I wanted Mark as a partner, or even a husband. I just knew I wanted him around – for ever. I think Hilary always believed that we'd end up together, and I knew that Les thought we should. I hadn't considered it because, when I met him, I was totally besotted with Rob. Mark, as I'd said to Hilary on more than one occasion, was just Mark. The one thing I did know was that I couldn't bear the thought of losing him – whether that was as a friend or part-time lover or something more. I didn't know if it would be enough to have him as a friend. If he suddenly announced he was marrying his actress, I really wasn't sure how I'd feel.

But suddenly, I think I did. In that instant I realized that if he married Melanie, his friendship alone would not be enough. I would feel as if I had totally lost him. Right now was not a great time for this sort of soul-searching! I was supposed to be sorting things out with Sarah, but it was because of Mark that this conversation was happening, and I couldn't push the thoughts out of my mind.

I could have completely screwed up his head over the years; first with the intensity of my relationship with Rob, and then almost drifting into the one with Derek, while Mark remained the only constant, which I had taken for granted. Maybe he had only gone along with what I wanted, and how I behaved, to keep me close. Perhaps he had finally got fed up with waiting for this flighty woman to really notice that Mark existed in his own right. Perhaps he'd finally tired of waiting for me to want him – as him – not as a prop for other failed relationships. Had he really now decided to go down a separate route? I did not like that possibility at all.

I glanced back at Sarah. She had a slightly triumphant expression on her face, as if she'd won the argument that we weren't having. 'I really don't know,' I said, at last.

She looked a trifle deflated. I think that maybe she had assumed my long hesitation in answering was due to me wondering how she would react to a reply that confirmed her assumptions. Perhaps if that had been my reply, and she believed I was going to run off with Mark, she may have reacted as she had this morning by flaring up with a question about what they were going to do now. If that was how my life was about to pan out, I think she would see it as a safe bet that I wouldn't offer to have someone else's kids in tow as well, and she would have had another reason to try to make me feel guilty. Now I imagined she couldn't ask that question, because the reply had become totally dependent on how much I wanted them in my life, and how much I liked them.

Part of me wanted to flare up too, to shout at her that it had always been dependent on what I wanted. Guilt didn't enter into it. They were Derek's kids, not mine. I had nothing to feel guilty about, anyway. He hadn't asked me to care for them. They just happened to have been in my house when he died. I could have phoned social services and got rid of them instantly, but I chose not to. I had grown to like them, not out of guilt, or out of pity, but just because I had. If I chose to look after them it would only be because I wanted to, not out of some sense of duty. I also wanted to shout at her that I'd like her a lot more if she stopped trying to make me feel guilty, and that if I did choose to look after them, I'd do it with or without Mark. If that was to be my choice, and he wanted me in his life – permanently – he'd just have to put up with having them there as well.

I shouted nothing. I just knew, in that instant, that if I had, it would have been, 'Help!' And it would have been to Hilary.

My head was swimming, and through the turmoil I remembered that there was another problem I needed to discuss as well. I unashamedly used it an excuse for changing the subject. 'Your grandparents will be back soon, and they want to talk to us.'

The fight drained out of her. 'What about?' She sounded genuinely frightened.

'I don't know.' I'd had an awful lot of 'don't knows' today.

'But they *are* your only relatives, apart from Uncle James. Perhaps they feel they have a responsibility towards you.'

'I doubt it,' she replied, with a slight rekindling of the fighting spirit. 'They're probably after some money!'

'Actually, that was my first thought.'

For the first time that day, she gave me a slight smile.

'But you never know, they may feel they let their daughter – your mum – down, and they'd like a chance to make up for that.'

She pulled a face. 'They're not likely to change. Mum did talk a bit about her childhood; it was pretty grim. It sounded as if they treated her like a slave. They'd brought her into the world, so she should be grateful and do everything for them as a thank you – that sort of thing. Mum left home as soon as she could. I really couldn't believe that she was still prepared to see them when she got older, or even wanted to! She always said that forgiveness was important.'

'It is important. And whatever problems they had, they were still her parents.'

'*I'll* never forgive them!'

'You never know, you might do one day, because you need to, but I can understand how you feel at the moment.'

'I don't want to see them.' She looked at me pleadingly.

'Okay, no one's going to make you.'

'Are you sure?'

'I am absolutely sure. Sarah, we may have had our disagreements, but I wouldn't do that to you.'

She looked at me for a moment, then her eyes dropped. 'We all have a file at school with our next of kin on it. You know, who to contact in an emergency. I'll have to put them on that now, won't I?'

'No, you won't. You can put whoever you like.'

'But it's them or Uncle James, isn't it?'

I smiled a sad smile. 'Your dad told the hospital I was his next of kin. I don't know the legal side of it, but that's what he said. I'm sure you can put down who you want, you don't have to be related.'

I think she was too afraid to ask the next question, so I answered it for her. 'Put me on your file.'

The front doorbell rang. Just as we might have been about to continue with that very fragile discussion on where her and her brother's future lay, we were interrupted. I found myself thinking that occasionally life was kind, as I went to open the door. Both my best friends were standing on the step together.

'Are you all right?' Hilary asked.

I nodded.

She ushered Tony inside. 'I've bought the things you needed, and some sandwiches for lunch, which should have been hours ago, so the choice was rubbish, plus a few gallons of alcohol.'

'Bless you.'

Mark grinned at me. 'I'll come in for a gallon, then.'

'How did you get on?'

'All sorted.'

'Really?'

'The insurance will pay for most of it.'

'And the rest?'

'Not your problem. I said I'd sort it.'

'What did you promise them at the bungalow?'

'The earth, just like you would have done.'

I laughed. 'But that includes all my time, no doubt?'

He took me by the shoulders. 'No, it doesn't. You were going to have some time off. You still are.'

'Only till next Thursday.'

'That's time enough.'

'But we were starting another job!'

'So, I've delayed that one a little bit, and the one after a bit more, and the one after...'

I aimed a punch at him, then grabbed hold of him and gave him a huge, clinging hug.

Oh, dear God, I said to the heavens, what *am* I going to do if he leaves me?

Chapter 32

'Look, it's that bird again!' Tony's voice made us all turn to the direction he was pointing. A pheasant was trotting down the lawn, at a rapid pace.

'Hey, that's pretty good, dinner's delivering itself,' Mark said.

'Sure, if you want to wait days while we hang it in the shed, till it turns green and starts stinking!'

Tony looked horrified.

'And you've got to shoot it first, and wring its neck if you haven't killed it,' Mark added.

Tony looked even more horrified.

'I bet you couldn't even shoot it,' Hilary joined in.

'I bet I could! I'd have got that one this morning.'

'One flew out of the bushes this morning, when…' I stopped. I didn't want to say, 'when we were searching for Sarah'. '…when we were in the garden.'

We were all sitting having drinks in the lounge, and the atmosphere was as good as it could be. I didn't want to ruin it. Sarah was quiet, but she had accepted a glass of wine and hadn't declined joining us all. No doubt she had a lot of thinking to do, following our conversation, although it was more likely to be the things that hadn't been said that were on her mind.

'So you reckon you could hit what you wanted with a gun, eh?' I said to Tony.

'Yeah!'

I winked at Hilary and left the room, returning a few moments later with an air rifle and a tin of pellets.

'Oh, cool! Can I really have a go?'

The whole idea of sitting having a peaceful drink vanished. Mark ran down the garden and placed his beer can on the ground.

'Hey, Mark, bring it back and fill it with water.'

He jogged back, drained his glass of beer, opened another can and tipped the contents in, and then headed off with two water-filled targets. Tony was hopping from one foot to the other, eager to get his hands on the gun. I showed him, very carefully, how to break the gun and insert a pellet, and made sure he wasn't pointing it at anyone, before ensuring he had it tight to his shoulder. He missed.

'Can I try again?'

'Let someone else have a go first.'

'Right, my turn.'

'It's my gun. It's my turn.' I hit the can and a thin stream of water spurted out of the side. There was a cheer from the others.

Hilary hit the second can, with the same effect. She and I had played at this on many occasions, and we both would have been very annoyed if we'd missed.

Mark took the gun and hit the second can lower down. Water appeared, to another cheer. Tony was beside himself with impatience, but I turned round to Sarah.

'Do you want to try?'

She shook her head.

Tony grabbed the gun eagerly, but he missed again. I could see a serious sulk coming on.

'Go on, have another go. Line up that little notch, there, so it's right in the middle of the circle of the sight on the end, and get them in line with the can.'

He frowned in deep concentration. He'd forgotten to clamp the butt into his shoulder, so it gave him quite a kick, but the can flew backwards with his shot.

Everyone gave him a huge cheer and he grinned happily, rubbing his shoulder.

'Okay, next round is in the kneeling position.'

Mark went down the garden and repositioned the targets, and the firing restarted. I looked round to ask Sarah to join us again, but she'd gone. Perhaps she wasn't interested, but I was more convinced that it was the frivolity from which she'd walked away.

The whole game became even more frivolous as we decided the third round was prone and dragged the rug outside to lie on. Mark had sent Tony off round the garden looking for some lumps of wood as new targets, and then Hilary had drawn daft faces on them. Wherever Sarah had gone, she must have still been able to hear the shouts and the laughter. If she couldn't cope with everyone having a good time, hiding from it wasn't going to help. Suddenly my thoughts turned to apprehension. Maybe she couldn't still hear the laughter.

'Back in a minute!' I called out. I didn't want to alarm anyone else. I felt the tension drain away as I found her sitting, reading, in her bedroom.

'Sometimes it helps to try to have some fun, even if you don't feel like it.'

'It doesn't seem right.'

'Life does go on, you know.'

'Well, you seem to be able to manage that, all right!'

We were back to argumentative mode.

'Ally, it's your go!'

'Okay, I'll skip this round. Won't be long!' I shouted back.

I sat on the bed. I was getting a bit angry, now.

'I miss Derek too. I have lost him, and I've lost other people in my life, as well. There are some losses that we never get over; they take a part of our lives with them, but somehow we have to make the best of the bits we've got left.'

I was tempted to say, At least he died. You don't have to deal with rejection as well!

'We may laugh and muck around, but it doesn't mean we've forgotten. The memories stay with us, and they're good memories. Yes, they can be sad at times, and that's as it should be, but we can't be sad all the time. It's the last thing your dad would have wanted.'

'I don't think he'd have wanted you to rush off and sleep with Mark.'

'Oh, don't start all that again. I am very fond of you, both of you, but you're not making it easy for me. I will do all I can, but I need your help as well.'

'All you can, with restrictions?'

'Yes. With restrictions. Your dad set restrictions too, remember? Otherwise you'd have had a summer holiday some time in the last umpteen years!' I got up. 'I'm going back to have a laugh, if I still can. Take it or leave it.'

I desperately tried to reattach the smile when I got downstairs, but it was a lot harder now. Mark and Hilary both realized where I'd gone, and Hilary raised her eyebrows at me in question. I just shrugged.

'I'd better go,' Mark said, looking at his watch.

'We can carry on, can't we?' Tony would have gone on all night.

'We can do it again tomorrow, if you want. We ought to do some work on the house in the afternoon. Phil and Andy will be here and they are really mean shots!'

'Oh, right, cool!'

Mark moved off towards the door.

'Are you seeing Melanie?' I kicked myself. I didn't ask him those sorts of questions, and it was the second time in two days.

'I'm seeing her, but she's not seeing me.' He smiled at my frown. 'I thought that I'd better go and see this stupid play. It's their last night here, then they're taking it on tour round the country. She's got a last-night party afterwards, to which I haven't been invited.'

I never questioned him about his social life, and he never gave out that much information. I hadn't lost him, yet.

Hilary, to my immense relief, was obviously not leaving. She helped me prepare a meal for four, while Tony got under our feet. There was little in the house in the way of games that would keep him entertained, and I was certainly not going to let him play with the gun alone, so I sent him out in the garden to find some smaller bits of wood. When I mentioned that my brothers would want to throw them up in the air and shoot at them, he was very willing to go. He disappeared and Hilary gave me a hug.

'We'll shut ourselves in the study later and talk,' I said.

'Absolutely. I will have to go home though. I must visit my mum tomorrow, and I'm off to San Francisco on Wednesday, remember.'

'I keep forgetting that. Sorry. You will say hi to your sister for me, won't you? It's years since I've seen her. How's she doing out there?'

'Loving it, she wouldn't come back now if we paid her.'

'Why would you want her to? It's a ready-made holiday.'

'Certainly is. So, when are you coming with me? She really would love to see you.'

'How about Wednesday?'

Hilary burst out laughing.

Sarah came at once when called for dinner, but she was subdued and didn't really join in any chat. Tony made up for her reticence. No one else got a chance to say much. We finished eating and everyone helped clear up. Sarah offered to make coffee, which was good of her, and I announced that I needed to talk to Hilary and told the kids they could put on the television if they wanted. If they were going to fight over what to watch, there was another set in the kitchen.

I shut the study door firmly and flopped into a chair.

'You look exhausted.'

'I am.'

'Come on, then, fill in all the details.'

I had explained as much as I could to Hilary, about the last few days, with a couple of phone calls, but so much seemed to have happened recently, it felt more like a month that had passed. I related, as accurately as I could recall, all my recent conversations, both with the kids and with Mark. Once I started talking, it was an absolute outpouring. I talked, I cried, I admitted my fears, and my faults, and eventually I stopped, feeling completely drained.

Hilary had said very little, except for the odd prompt or question about precisely how I'd felt. Now she stared at me.

After a long silence, I said to her, 'Please don't tell me I'm a stupid cow.'

She smiled. 'I think you're a very mixed-up one.'

'I don't know what to do.'

'I know, but I can't tell you. Only your heart can do that.'

Chapter 33

I turned over and looked at the bedside clock yet again. It hadn't even moved along five minutes since I'd last looked. My eyes were too tired to let me read my book, but the thoughts swirling round in my head wouldn't let me sleep. 'Oh, sod it,' I muttered and got out of bed.

Having succeeded in getting down the stairs in the dark, I pushed the lounge door closed before switching on the wall lights. It was a warm night, so I opened the patio doors and turned the outside lights on as well. I poured a drink and sat on the sofa, letting the gentle night breeze drift into the room. The sleep that had eluded me in bed crept up on me.

'Mum?'

I awoke instantly. It wasn't Tony's voice. Sarah moved hesitantly into the room.

'What's wrong?'

There were traces of tears in her eyes. 'Mum,' she said again, very softly. 'I think there might be an aardvark in the garden.'

I stared at her, feeling the tears beginning to prick at my own eyes. 'I tell you what,' I answered, 'I think he'll hang around while you come over here and give me a big hug.'

She ran across the room and wrapped her arms around me. I hugged her with more emotion than time had ever granted me the chance to find with her father. She sobbed onto my shoulder and I wept silently with her, and for her, and for me.

The lights must have disturbed Tony because suddenly he appeared in the doorway. 'What's going on?'

Sarah started to move, but I held one arm firmly around her shoulders and kept her sitting beside me.

He glanced from us to the open garden doors. 'What are you doing?'

"We're waiting for the aardvark.'

I held out my other arm and he came readily and eagerly across the room, to join this strange, new family union that fate had created for all of us.